the woman in the woods

je rowney

Other works by this author:

Charcoal
The Derelict Life of Evangeline Dawson
Ghosted
I Can't Sleep

The Lessons of a Student Midwife Series
Life Lessons
Love Lessons
Lessons Learned

The On Call Midwife at Christmas

©2021 All rights reserved

This book or parts thereof may not be reproduced in any form, stored in any retrieval system, or transmitted in any form by any means—electronic, mechanical, photocopy, recording, or otherwise—without prior written permission of the publisher.

This is a work of fiction. Names, characters, businesses, places, events, locales, and incidents are either the products of the author's imagination or used in a fictitious manner. Any resemblance to actual persons, living or dead, or actual events is purely coincidental.

A man and a woman. A cabin in the woods. A ghost story.

You think you've heard all this before.

You think you know what I'm going to tell you.

This is not what you think it is.

This is not the same old story.

I know, because this happened to me.

- Seb Archer

Chapter One

"You're a fucking asshole."

There she is, the love of my life.

"Sebastian Archer, you are a fucking asshole."

I don't even bother looking up.

I'm not an asshole. Not really. Then again, sometimes I am.

"What this time?" I ask, even though I already know.

I'm Seb Archer. You might have heard of me, but only if you are interested in poker. That's what I do. That's who I am. I would love to tell you that I'm a man of many talents, but poker is all I have ever been good at.

I had a "proper job" once. I was in sales. I was That Guy. The one who cold calls you at three on a Saturday afternoon when you're settling down to watch television. It sucked the life out of me. I volunteered in a soup kitchen for a while, I thought that *giving something back* to the community would make me feel better, but it got me down. That's the kind of selfish prick I am. I couldn't commit to helping people because it made *me* feel bad.

Katie is, of course, an angel. She's a care assistant, so she spends most of her time doing things for other people that they can't do for themselves. She works in an old folks' home about a half hour from Harborough where we live. It's a sweet little village and I'm sure they are sweet little ladies and gentlemen, but her job is my worst nightmare.

"You were meant to be home early last night so we could spend some time together today."

I was. I said that. When I said it, I probably meant it, but I was running bad, I was deep in the hole, and I had to play my way out of it. I was at the poker table, and I had to stay there. When you're down a couple of bags, and a massive whale rocks up, there's only one thing to do: put your hand in your pocket, pull out your wallet, and get your money on the table.

Don't worry about the jargon, it doesn't matter. I was losing. That's all you need to know. I was losing and then a terribly rich terrible player showed up to bail me out. My hero. Thank you.

Katie doesn't care about that though. She cares that I came home at seven, slept until three and missed our wonderful morning of quality time together.

Dexter comes bounding in, straight up onto the bed, all paws and fur and tongue, making sure I'm not going to be getting back to sleep. He's not allowed up here, but he doesn't give a toss about that, and today neither do I.

"Down. Get down," Katie whines. "Seb get him down." She's doing nothing useful, standing there at the foot of the bed, pouting.

Dexter is nuzzling into me, paws outstretched, lying alongside me, his body pressed against mine. He's nearly as tall as me, stretched out like this. Katie wanted a little dog, something like a Yorkie or a Chihuahua that she could put stupid clothes on and carry in her handbag. She wanted an accessory rather than a pet. I didn't want a dog at all, which put me in the driving seat.

Obviously, we got Dexter, but as I would only agree to it if we got a Lab, in a way I won. I'd love to tell you that Katie gave up on her dreams of dressing up her doggo when we bought him, but no. She tried to get him into a sweater, and he destroyed it in about five minutes. Strangely when she tried him with a jaunty bandana, he tipped his head to the side and let it be. I managed to get it off him and lose it on our next walk.

'No dogs on the bed' was my rule. I wanted to keep this place exclusively for sleep. Okay, and the other thing we do here, sometimes, but mostly just for sleep. Dexter has his own bed down in the kitchen. He spends most of his day down in front of the Aga, so it makes sense to leave his bed there at night.

At this moment, I couldn't care less.

"Seb!" I get the blame, of course. Katie could have shut the door, she could shout at Dexter rather than at me, but somehow it's my fault.

I roll onto my belly and bury my face into the pillow. I've had, what, well okay, I've probably had my eight hours of sleep now. I guess it's time I got up. I exhale, long and hard. Perhaps if I pushed my face in further, I could suffocate myself and not have to deal with Katie anymore. Dexter pokes his muzzle into my side and licks just below my ribs. He probably read my mind.

"Good boy," I say, my voice muffled into the soft cotton.

I push up and roll back over, ruffling his fur before sitting up to look at Katie.

"Yeah," I say. "Sorry about today."

"Sorry? You're sorry? How many times, exactly, are you going to be sorry?"

It's a reasonable enough question, but the way that she squeals the words doesn't make it sound particularly reasonable.

"Katie. Poker isn't just my hobby, it's my job. It's my life. I have to stay late sometimes." Her expression is becoming increasingly irritated. "Even when I don't want to," I add, reaching out to her. "Come here," I say. "Come on."

"You could leave at any time. You don't get in trouble from your boss if you clock out early. I thought that's why you wanted to play in the first place. You didn't want to be told what to do. You said it would be easier, that you would have more freedom. Is this freedom? Is this a better life?"

For the most part, yes, my life does give me a lot more freedom than I had when I worked in sales. There is the odd time, like this, when my life is far more complicated than it would be with a nine-to-five.

"I've had enough of it, Seb. Enough. You promised me that today was our time. You promised that we could do something together. I don't ask a lot of you…" She does. "…but if we don't ever see each other then what are we doing here? Why are we wasting our time?"

Dexter is as close to me as he can get. Like a child whose parents are fighting, he nuzzles into me, looking for comfort and reassurance.

"It's okay," I say. "Everything's going to be okay." I'm using my softest, most gentle voice, and Katie thinks I am speaking to her.

"It's not going to be okay unless you start to make an effort. You need to do what you say you will do. Start keeping your promises. Think about someone else other than yourself for once. Just for once. Can you do that? Can you even do that?"

She's crying now, and trembling, her voice shaking, her shoulders rising and falling with her rapid, light breaths.

"Shit. Katie. Come on, please. Come and sit down. Let's talk about it."

"I'm done with talking. All you ever do is talk. All you ever give me are words. I've had enough."

I run my hand along Dexter's back, his fur comforting me as much as I am comforting him.

"Katie…"

"Don't you 'Katie' me." Maybe this is it. Maybe this is the end. "I've had it."

"Katie." I don't know what else to say, and repeating her name really isn't helping. "What do you want me to do? What do I need to say? What is it that you want?"

"I want us to be happy. I want things to be like they used to be."

That. Well, that sounds so easy, doesn't it?

"I want to be happy too," I say. It's the most obvious thing in the world, but maybe sometimes we forget.

"I want us to be happy together." She moves closer and settles on the end of the bed. "Do you think we can be?"

"Sure. Of course we can."

"Not if we never see each other. Not if you keep letting me down like this."

We could carry on for hours, going around in circles, or I could surrender now. I've only been awake for ten minutes and I really don't have the energy to fight with her. As always, I take the easy option. "Tell me what I can do to make it better, and I will do it."

She is still glowering at me, so I put on my best smile, all teeth and sparkly eyes, the kind of smile that always gets her. I'm not the most handsome man, but I'm fairly attractive when I work my best assets. I know how to get to her, so I put on my best show. "Hey, babe. Really. Come on. I'm sorry. Whatever you want, say it. I'll do better from now on, I promise."

Her frosty glare starts to melt. "I don't…I mean I shouldn't trust you. Not after all the times you let me down…"

Before she can slip back into that loop again, I shuffle across the bed towards her, gently hutching Dexter out of the way. I sidle up to her, wrap my arms around her, and pull her close. I know from experience that this is one of the other things that she particularly likes: being caught up in a big bear hug. At first, she remains tense, but I start to stroke her hair and she softens against me. Dexter has moved to take his place beside me, and he's trying to get in on the action, rubbing against us. I keep my arms around Katie.

"Anything you want, Pie. Anything."

"Oh Bun Bun."

There. She's reverted to the pet name that I despise, so everything is obviously going to be alright.

I kiss the top of her head. I think that we are done and back on track, but no, there is more.

"I want to go away somewhere," she says.

I wasn't prepared for this. I didn't think there would actually be conditions to the surrender.

"Away?" I stutter the word.

"Yeah, away." She pulls back from me and takes hold of my hands in hers. Her expression has changed from abject misery and disappointment in me to one of…what…triumph? I'm starting to feel like I have been had.

I gulp in a breath.

"Anywhere in particular?"

"Somewhere that we can be alone together. Somewhere we can spend time together, just the two of us, with no distractions."

No poker. That's what she means. No casino. Nothing to keep me from spending time with her.

"But…"

"When you had a regular job, we used to go away all of the time."

"You had a regular job too then. You didn't work shifts like you do now. It was easier then."

"Easier, sure. But it's not impossible now. You're kind of self-employed, right?"

I guess you could see it that way, but when I am not playing, I am not making money. Apart from my bankroll, the amount of cash I have set aside for poker, I don't really have an awful lot.

I nod and shrug in one movement.

"So, take some time off. If this relationship is important to you."

There's the ultimatum. I knew it would come. Poker or Katie.

It's just a few days. She's not asking me to give up forever, and I appreciate that, but...

She tilts her head to the side, in much the same way that Dexter does when waiting for me to do something. Then she gives me that huge beaming Katie-smile that always gets me. Her face lights up, her eyes are so beautiful. She's the kind of perfect that I don't deserve, and here I am not even willing to give up a few days to make her happy. To make *us* happy.

I realise that I am being a selfish dick.

"I've been a selfish dick," I say. "Sure. Let's go somewhere. Let's work things out. We can be happy, Pie." I bend forwards to kiss her, but she reaches out and places her finger onto my lips.

"This is our last chance, Sebastian. If we can't get it together, I think we should give up."

"I…" I try to talk but she shakes her head.

"All the girls think that I should have already left you a long time ago, so…" She shrugs. "We make it work or we let it go."

I instinctively look at Dexter and he looks back at me with his huge chocolate brown eyes.

I nod. "Okay."

Chapter Two

Katie found this place. It's billed as a romantic getaway, but to me it looks like a cabin in the middle of nowhere. I left all the planning to her. Once she gets an idea in her head, she's like a dog with a bone. As soon as I agreed to it, she was on the internet, searching for *her* ideal mini-break location. Whether or not it was somewhere that I would like to spend a week of my life really doesn't matter. She doesn't wear the pants in our relationship, don't get me wrong. We have always been a democratic couple, or at least I like to kid myself that this is true.

The nearest casino to the village is seventy miles away. Yes, I checked. You can bet that Katie checked too. If I can't get to a casino then I have to spend my evenings with her. Just because I checked doesn't mean that I would have tried to skip out on her. I agreed to this break. I've put five years into this, nearly six, and I'm not a quitter. When the cards run against you, you don't stand up, leave the table and quit. No. You keep playing. You know that it is going to get better. If you keep making the right moves at the right time, then it's going to get better. I'm committed to this relationship in the poker sense of the word just as much as the emotional sense. I'm not giving up.

The road to the cabin takes us through Culloton. It's one of those nowhere places. A name on a map. A village you'd only be aware of if you were a local. The village is not on any route to anywhere. The curtains are closed in the tiny windows of the tiny terraced cottages that line the narrow road. The streetlights seem dimmer here than they do back home. I'd like to say that it's atmospheric, but really it feels plain eerie, like any minute a fog is going to descend and zombies are going to come thundering down the road. The image isn't helped by the creepy ass sign that hangs outside the only building with a light on.

Something about it catches my attention.

"Watch the road!" Katie says, nudging me unnecessarily as I turn my head to do a double take.

"Weird name for a pub." I nod my head towards the rear-view mirror.

She shuffles around in her chair to look over her shoulder.

"Not really," she says, sounding disappointed. Disappointed in me, not disappointed by the pub.

Disappointed that I raised her expectations. You'd think she would be used to it.

'The Woman in the Woods'. Maybe it's not such a weird name, but something about it gave me a chill. Must have been my melodramatic, zombie-creating brain at work. If you have a dull life and dull thoughts, you have to start making things up.

"Maybe we can come down for drinks one night?" I take a shot at turning things around.

Katie grunts a response that could mean yes or no. I give up.

She's got her feet up on the dashboard now. I've told her, more than once, not to do that, but she doesn't listen. That's a lie. She clearly did listen, because she's taken her shoes off. Instead of her dirty Birkenstocks, she's resting her bare soles on the dash. She's got the seat pushed back as far as it will go, but she's still scrunch-folded, trying to fit into position in the tiny space.

I can't let myself get too pissed off about it; I'm concentrating on the road, trying to work out where the turning is. My satnav has already given up trying to guide me. The satellite connection is almost non-existent out here.

"Hey," Katie says. She jabs a finger into my arm like a small blunt dagger. "Hey," she repeats as she prods.

I take a hand off the wheel and bat at her as if she were a mosquito.

"Quit it." I glance at her quickly, looking for long enough to catch her expression. That miserable sulky look I've come to know and hate. That look is one of the reasons we are here.

"Answer me then," she buzzes.

I take a deep breath and try to remember what it was that she asked me.

"Katie, I didn't hear you. I'm sorry. I'm just trying to work out where the fuck we are going." I sound even more irritated than I am, and I am pretty fucking irritated right now.

Another deep breath. This is meant to be our *Last Chance Holiday*. I don't want to start it like this.

"Honey, I'm sorry. Just getting a bit stressed by these directions. I'm sorry, babe." I reach over to put my hand onto her leg.

This time she's the one to push me away. We do this. Play this game of who's on top, who's in control, who has the power in this ridiculous thing that we call a relationship.

I suck it up.

"I'll make it up to you when we get there. Whatever you like. You name it."

Give her some more power. She can't fight against that. Clever little move, isn't it?

It works. She pulls her feet down, tucks her legs back into the footwell and sits up straight as a rod.

"Anything?"

"Anything, Pie."

Pie. I hate that nickname. I hate that I ever created it.

I can tell that she's smiling but I don't bother looking over to see. I know how this all works.

"So, what was it you said, Pie?"

She makes a tiny "hmm" sound, which is the audible translation of a shrug.

"Doesn't matter now," she says.

All that animosity for a "*doesn't matter now*". Standard.

We're out of the village now, just fields to either side. I can see the woods ahead. The horizon is a low hill, and the trees stand along it like a phalanx, ready to crest and charge. We should have set off from home earlier, of course. I wanted to leave by half past one but instead Katie delayed and dawdled, and we finally set off at three. The sun is melting in the sky, turning it a pale orange shimmer. Katie has a round circle of blusher in our bathroom just that colour. It's sunlight, but still, it feels cold.

We are heading in the right direction. I know that now. We must be, because the road is taking us into the shade of the woodland. Strands of ochre light leak between the shadow tendrils of trees.

I flick my eyes over to the clock. It's nearly seven thirty. We said we would meet the key-holder at eight. Despite leaving late we are going to be on time. You'd think I knew that Katie Pie was going to drag her heels. I told her we needed to set off an hour and a half before we actually needed to leave because she is predictably annoying.

I've had the radio on the whole way, but now we're getting closer I turn it down a couple of notches, trying to concentrate.

I'm looking out for a turn-off, but I'm not sure how far it's going to be.

"I was listening to that," Katie says. I can hear the pout in her tone.

"Honey, could you help me look for the road to the cabin, please? It should be on your side." If I don't answer her, and give her something to do instead, it might work. Especially if I give her an important task.

"Sure," she says.

That earns her a smile. I turn my head to give it to her, and she smiles back.

Her smile was one of the things that drew me to her in the first place. She worked behind the counter at the Coffee Express where I fed my caffeine addiction on my commute. Bang between the station and my office. There's a stand on the platform, and I used to always stop there. Straight off the 08:20 and up to the counter, reusable cup in hand, ready for my extra-hot-extra-shot latte. One day it was closed, and I cursed a little and walked the two hundred meters to the next franchised outlet. You're never more than two hundred metres from a Coffee Express. That should be their tag line.

"I said, 'Is that the one?'" Katie nudges me, harder than she needs to.

"What?" I was lost in the past. Back in the day that I could have made a different decision and never met her. What would I be doing now if that hole in the wall had been open? Would I be on a *Last Chance Holiday* with someone else? Probably. In all of my previous breakups there has been one common denominator - me. Of course, I hear you say, but what I mean is that I'm usually the cause of everything bad that happens.

"The turning," she says. The whine is back. It never stays away long.

I missed it. I wasn't concentrating. My mind was on other things. So often it seems that this is the case.

"Shit," I mutter. I don't quite slam on the brakes, but I press down harder than I should, and we squeal to a stop. My eyes flash to the rear-view mirror, which, arguably I should have checked before slowing, but it's fine. The road is clear. Clear behind. Clear ahead.

"Seb!" We have already stopped before she starts to complain. It's an unnecessary add-on.

"Sorry, Pie." Her pet name might as well be that. '*Sorry Pie*'. It's what I seem to say all the time.

I look up and down the road again before attempting to execute a three-point turn. The road is narrower than I had calculated, and my three-point turn ends up being a five-pointer. Katie is silent but I can feel the resentment oozing from her.

I start to drive, more slowly now, heading back the way we just came.

"Keep your eyes open this time," Katie says.

"Okay, honey. Where was it? How far back?"

"Not far. It was quite narrow."

"You're sure it was the turning?"

"It was *a* turning. Is there more than one? Was there some special turning I was meant to be looking for?"

"The keyholder said head down here and take the first turning to the left, so yes, if you saw a turning, that's the one."

"*If* I saw it?"

"You did see it. I'm not saying you didn't see it. I just mean…"

She's holding up her hand like a stop sign. I can just see it from the corner of my eye, and I don't turn to see more.

I want to sigh but I know it will just escalate to more of an argument.

Instead, I drive. My eyes alternate between the road ahead and the tree line to my right, looking for the break that indicates the track.

It's twenty-five to eight. Still plenty of time. I'm moderately calm, considering.

She turns the volume dial up, and I furrow my brow. It's not helping. What is it about the car radio that makes it so much more difficult to work out where I'm going with it blaring out? In fairness, I know where I'm going. Dead ahead.

Even at a crawl-speed, I'm about to pop out of the woods back onto the open road before I know it.

"You missed it again?" Katie blows a bubble with the chewing gum that she's just pulled out of her pocket. It snaps as it pops. I hate the smell of it. It's that fruity gum, if it were mint, I could tolerate it. She knows I hate it.

"Did you see it?"

"Not that time. I wasn't really looking though. I thought you were."

"Jeez, Katie. Help me out here. What's wrong with you?"

"What's wrong with ME? You missed the turning twice and it's my fault?"

Here we go.

We are twenty minutes away from the start of our holiday but only seconds away from disaster. I could choose to retaliate, or I can take the blame, and get on with it. I know what I want to do, but I bite my tongue.

"We still have plenty of time. Don't worry, Pie. Could you have a look out with me this time, please?"

She replies as though I asked her to pull out her own teeth with pincers. "Okay. Drive slowly though. And look this time."

"Okay, Pie. Okay."

I turn the car around again and head out of the last rays of the day's sun into the dark of the woods once more.

This journey is the perfect metaphor for our relationship. Constantly battling and going around in circles. You may wonder why I think it is worth it to even try to save whatever we have. I wonder the same things sometimes, but you know how relationships are. I suppose I remember that woman I met in the coffee shop. I remember her smile, and I remember going back, day after day, long after the hole in the wall on the station platform reopened, just to see that smile. I believe that the woman she was then still exists. The woman sitting next to me, pulling chewing gum from her mouth in a long string and twisting it around her finger is still the same woman, somewhere inside. I know she is. Things can be what they were. We can be happy. We were happy.

"Here. Stop!"

Can I just concentrate for ten seconds? I can see why she gets annoyed with me. I understand, really, I do.

I engage the brake just before we get to the turning, flick on the indicator as a reflex more than a requirement. The roads have been clear of other traffic since we left the village.

"Thanks, honey," I say, and gently pat her warm thigh.

She's wearing a flowery tea dress. She looks cute in it, don't get me wrong, but it's hardly the kind of thing you wear out in the woods. I suggested jeans and boots, but she grimaced and shook her head, and that was the end of the conversation. When she's cold later it will be my fault. I'm sure she will find a reason to blame me.

"Not so hard to see, is it?" she says, and again I resist the temptation to verbally lash out at her.

"Thanks for finding it." I pull my hand from her leg and swing the car onto the track that should lead us to the cabin.

It's a dry, sandy track, and pea-sized gravel chips plink against the sides of the car as I drive. I wince, imagining the chipped paintwork. It's not a new car, but I try to look after it all the same. I don't really have the money to replace it, or even shell out for a new paint job. I slow down, trying to limit the damage, and Katie notices immediately.

"We're going to be late. What are you stopping for?"

"I'm not *stopping*, hon. This track is tearing up the paintwork. I got to slow down."

"It's I *have* to slow down. Not I *got* to."

I wipe my mouth with the back of my hand, turn toward her, about to speak, and, just in time, I manage to stop myself. I give her a smile that I hope is more cute than cloying and turn my eyes back to the road.

"Nearly there, Pie. Can't want to see this place." I don't have to feign enthusiasm. I am actually looking forward to staying in this cabin. The idea of being out in the woods, back to nature and all that, it reaches out to a part of me. Kind of like playing Boy Scouts or Bear Grylls or something. There's a manly vibe to retreating to nature, isn't there? And being with Katie, well, of course. Yeah. Whatever.

I'm not saying that I already know how this is going to go, but I have a pretty good idea. Do Last Chance Holidays ever end up with the couple working things out and going home to a happily ever after? If they do then I haven't heard it. Do I want things to work out with Katie? Do I ask myself why I'm bothering?

The track is long, but even in the dim light I can see where we are headed.

It's narrow, just a single lane bordered on both sides by trees, right up to the edge of the shingle. The overhang drops low, forming a canopy. It's claustrophobic, stifling.

The woodland is dense, but ahead, way ahead, I can see a clearing. I can see light. The literal light at the end of the almost tunnel.

"You see it, Pie?" I wave my hand and the window, look at her again and give her another of those smiles.

She's about to reply when there's a sickening THUCK sound and the car judders.

I didn't see anything run in front of us, but we definitely hit something. I look up to the rear view, then the side mirrors but it's too dark to make out anything on the road behind.

"Fuck." I step on the brake and pull over, even though *over* is essentially still the middle of the lane.

"Watch where you're going Seb! Fuck. What if that had been a deer or a bear or something?"

A bear. Where does she think we are? I want to laugh in her face but she's looking at me with a *"you could have killed the both of us you're a reckless maniac"* expression, and I really don't want to make this any worse.

"Oh, Pie." I say, and that's almost as bad. My tone of voice makes it come out wrong and her face contorts into an ugly screwed up ball of hatred. She's like that witch in the fairy story that uses magic to make her look like a beautiful queen. Underneath, when she shows her true self, she's gnarly and twisted. Just like me. Just like me.

Dexter is going nuts, and he makes a break for my door as soon as I start to open it.

"No," I say in a voice that is far harsher than I intended. It's not his fault. He gives me a questioning look, but stays in the back of the car Still, I open the door only enough to let me out, and make sure I shut it quickly behind me. We have almost made it. The last thing I need is Dexter running off chasing squirrels or whatever now. I step out into the lane. It's gritty sand, specked with tiny rocks, and I feel the crunch reverberate through me as I walk back the way we just drove.

I can see Dexter with his nose pressed up against the back window, leaving thick wet drool on the glass.

Katie winds her window down and shouts. "What was it? Can you just leave it? Let's just go."

Of course, she would think that. Leave it. Fuck whatever it was. She uses up all of her empathy in her job, she has none left for anything or anyone else.

I raise my hand in a half-*'wait'*, half-wave, and keep walking.

There's a furry lump on the track. It's not moving, but I can hear a sound coming from it. Not a loud howl, not an anguished snarl, just a low, grumbling hum. I get closer and start to pick out the detail. It's big, bigger than I thought. Black and white, or at least a dirty grey that I take to be white. It's only when I crouch next to it that I can really make out what it is that I am looking at, what it is that I hit. It's a badger. There's an angry, oozing split along his gut. His tiny sharp teeth are gritted against the pain he must be feeling. He must be because that sound is a hiss now, a wheeze of a noise that is taking everything he has to make. His front paw, the one closest to me, moves slightly, as though he is beckoning to me, signalling.

"Shit."

I stand up, run my fingers through my hair, look down the road at the car. I can see Dexter in the back window still, pressed against the glass. Katie has stopped looking at what's going on and I can make out the glow of the light from her mobile phone. She's occupying herself, catching up with the gossip, leaving me to deal with this. She's not even trying to settle Dexter. What did I expect?

That noise again. It's a gurgling plea. I know what I should do. I know there's no hope for this guy. I crouch again, reach out a hand towards him. Thoughts of rabies, teeth sinking into my flesh, danger to myself flash through my head and I pull it back again.

"Shit."

From a safe distance, I try to get a look at the damage, but it's futile.

I know what I should do.

There's only one way to help him now.

Beyond the car, only a few hundred feet ahead, I can see the lights of the cabin. We should be there now. I check my watch: 8:03. We were ahead of schedule; we were going to get there on time. And now, I am crouched beside a fucking badger instead of sinking the first of many cans.

"Okay," I say. "Okay."

I'm talking to the badger; I'm talking to myself. I kick a rock along the track in a vain attempt to release some of the tension, but it doesn't help.

"I'm sorry."

Even though I'm certain that the poor creature can't understand me, I mutter the words in a way that he can't hear them.

I stand up, turn, and walk back to the car.

Dexter tries to push his nose into the doorway as I open it to climb back inside, and I have to push him back. I throw Katie an accusing look. Couldn't she keep hold of him? Couldn't she do something, just one time?

"What was it?" she asks, not looking up from her phone.

I don't answer. I run my hand through my hair again, and then grab hold of the steering wheel, gripping it tightly, feeling that tension again.

"Seb?" Now she looks at me, but I don't look back.

I look into the rear-view mirror, slam the car into reverse and speed backwards up the track towards the badger.

The thud, this time, doesn't feel as bad.

"Seb!" Katie's voice is a shriek, like a fucking banshee. She reaches across and grabs hold of my left arm, and I almost skid the car off the road.

Dexter barks, in answer to Katie's noise or in fear for his life at her stupid carelessness.

"Fuck sake, Katie." I slam the brake and shake her off. "What do you want me to do? What am I meant to do?"

"You killed it! You KILLED it! Seb!"

If she had bothered to get out of the car, if she had seen it, she wouldn't be overreacting like this. If she had been a bit more interested in real life and less interested in what was happening on SnapShot, she wouldn't be freaking out, and freaking Dexter out.

"That's right," I say. I wanted to sound calm, but the calmness seems too much, almost psychotic in context.

"What's wrong with you? What the hell is wrong before you?" She's crying now. Great.

"Oh, what's right with me, Katie? Should we turn around now, go back home and forget about all of this bullshit?" Dexter is pushing his nose between the seats, between the two of us.

"You're upsetting Dexter. I did what I had to do, okay?"

Katie wipes at her face, running a finger under each eye to sweep away the black lines of mascara. She flips down the visor on her side and squints into the mirror. The light glares onto her face and I wonder for a second why I ever thought she was beautiful.

Dexter pushes his nose into my hand, and I turn down to him and force a smile. "Hey boy. It's okay. Everything's okay. We're nearly there now. Nearly there boy. Everything's okay. We're okay, Katie. It's okay."

She snorts a sob, flicks the visor back up, and wriggles in her seat, straightening up, getting herself together.

"Don't think you've heard the last of this, Sebastian."

I know I haven't. I know this one is going to be a long runner. What was I supposed to do?

We are moving again. Away from the mush in the road that was a badger, towards the light at the end of the track. Keep focussed. Ignore the woman sniffing and fake-crying to my left, the dog poking his nose anxiously through the gap between the seats. Focus. Ignore. That's what I do.

I'm thankful that it's not far. I don't know how much longer I could bear this.

Chapter Three

It's just gone ten past, nearly quarter past eight; we're not all that late. Still, we are late, and I hate it. I'm more stressed by our lateness than by the whining babble coming from Katie.

"Ssh," I say. "Ssh."

She flicks me a glance, but I know that she cares enough about what the stranger we are about to meet will think of her to fix her face before she steps out of the car.

Dexter is pushing his way forward, getting his legs up on the back of the seats, trying to jump over. He can't make it, and starts trying to squeeze his way between, through the too-small gap. He knows we have finally arrived. I'd rather send Katie off to walk him, stretch his legs, give the poor guy a break, give me a break from her, but we are already late. I don't want to drag this out any further.

"Hey boy. Calm down, Mister. Hey."

I rub his nose, ruffle the fur on top of his head, and he calms slightly. Only slightly. He wants to get out of here. I do too. Katie has got her make-up pouch out of her handbag, and she's brushing mascara onto her lashes. Great timing. Like she couldn't have done this further back down the line.

I pull the key out of the ignition and the light on her visor mirror fades.

"Seb!" she whines.

"You look..." I search for the right word. I want to get this right first time. "Perfect. You look perfect."

I can just about make out the shape of her in the glow that's coming from the light of the house. She looks like she always does. Still, I know she is smiling. My words had the right effect.

I reach back over to Dexter and click his lead into the silver loop on his thick red leather collar. He licks my hand as I pass it by his mouth. Warm but dry. I have to get him in, get him a drink then take him out for a piss.

I wipe off the drool and mutter to him, "Goodboygoodboytherenowgoodboy."

There's no bell on the heavy wooden door. The knocker is a black iron loop, and it sends a shockwave of noise as I lift it and let it fall twice in quick succession. Katie winces melodramatically and Dexter tilts his head to the side. It's colder than I had expected. I should have put my jacket on before we came to the house. I thought the keyholder would be waiting for us, anxious to hand over and be on his way. I look at Katie and she looks back. We wait.

Dexter stands up and stretches his legs again, like he doesn't know what to do with himself. He sniffs at a grid next to the stone brick wall, walks away as far as the lead will allow him, turns, and walks back.

"Knock again," Katie says.

"Wait. Give them chance."

I can hear sound from inside. A television. No. A radio. Voices talking, but definitely a radio. There's a difference in style, isn't there? The way a radio presenter speaks, it's not the same as a television programme. I can't hear what is being said, but the low hum of noise is there.

"Seb." Katie won't quit.

I raise my hand towards the knocker again, but before I can make contact, the door starts to open. I withdraw quickly, so I don't look like an impatient (late) prick.

Dexter pushes forward, eager to meet our host, always excited to make friends with someone new. I try to pull him back, but he's too quick for me. He's been coiled up all day on the journey and now I can't stop him from springing loose.

"Dexter! Oh God, I'm sorry. I mean, I'm sorry…shit."

So, there we go, I've taken the Lord's name in vain and mildly sworn in front of this guy already and I've only said one sentence. First impressions count, right?

He smiles, and I take a breath. He bends down and pets Dexter gently. "Hello boy. You must have had a long day."

The man is tall, heavily built, but not overweight. He's wearing a tweed jacket, shirt and jeans over what looks like a five-days-a-week gym-toned body. His eyes and hair are coal-black. He has all the basic features of a handsome man, but he is strikingly average-looking.

"We all have," Katie says. She has switched to charming mode, putting on her sweet smile and little girl lost voice. She knows how to impress people; I'll give her that. Maybe I should have stayed in the car and let her deal with this. She could have done all of the talking, checked us in, unpacked, made dinner, whatever, and I could have taken Dexter through the woods.

Maybe I wouldn't have come back.

"Come in, come in," the man says, stepping to the side. "You must be Sebastian and Katie."

No one ever addresses *her* by her full name, but it seems the default when people address me. Katherine. She hates it.

We walk into the hall and the wave of warmth from the open fire hits me immediately. I hadn't realised just how cold I was.

"Yes," she says, extending her hand. "Pleased to meet you."

She's courteous to a tee. She knows what to do, what to say.

I nod, and shake hands too, passing Dexter's lead over to my left hand.

"And this is…?"

"Dexter"

Dexter wags his tail ferociously at the mention of his name.

"Roman," the keyholder says. "Roman Blackheath."

I see Katie's eyes widen. She's so easily impressed. It's sickly.

"Roman. Hi. Great to meet you. So sorry we are late. We were nearly on time but…"

Katie cuts in before I start to go into detail about the roadkill. "We got a little lost. Missed the turning," she says.

"Well," Roman smiles. "I suppose if you don't know what you're looking for, you can drive right past it."

I nod again.

His accent is rhotic, drawling his *r* sounds in a plummy local accent, far removed from our own tones. It feels welcoming, warm, just like this room.

The cabin is as spectacular as the photos on the webpage made it out to be, which is always a pleasant surprise. Katie isn't even trying to conceal her awe, standing open-mouthed, her eyes darting around, taking it all in.

"Gorgeous, isn't it?" Roman says. "Come now. Don't let me stay in your way too long. Sebastian, can I get you to quickly sign in and then I'll hand over your key…keys?...and be out of your way. One key? Two?"

"Two," I say immediately. Katie flashes me a look, but I choose to ignore it. "I might need to take Dex out on my own, give the girl a lie-in." Truth is I don't want to be locked out if Katie throws a tantrum, but only Katie and I need to know that.

She fakes a smile, and Roman nods. "Of course. No problem."

Dexter is pulling anxiously at the lead now, but I don't want to let him free until Roman leaves. It's stupid really. We are going to be staying here for five days, perhaps I should start to let him feel at home now. With Roman still here though, I don't feel…what? Comfortable?

He places a sheet of paper down onto a small semi-circular writing table against the wall. The desk looks expensive, polished wood, perhaps mahogany; I'm not an expert on this sort of thing. The surface is felted, a heavy green cloth like a poker table. I try not to think about that.

"Just a few formalities," Blackheath says. "In case there are any breakages or losses or, well, in case anything goes terribly wrong. You can't hold me responsible." He smiles, and I am sure it is meant to be amiable.

"Well, I don't plan on losing anything," I say, trying to smile.

"No one ever does, do they?"

I scrawl my name across the bottom of the form and hand it back to Roman.

"Is this your cabin?" Katie asks, and for once I am happy to have her interruption. "Or are you just responsible for the rentals?"

"Oh yes," he says. "This whole area of woodland, from the main road out of the village, off on deep into the estate. All of it belongs to the Blackheath family." His voice drops off, and he looks like he is lost in thought. I'm about to say something when he snaps back into speech. "This cabin is one of my properties. One of my favourites."

Katie looks suitably impressed, of course, but I'm not enthralled by his arrogance. Okay, I'm jealous that he has all this, and I have a one-bedroomed garden flat in Harborough. Whatever.

"You live in the woods too then?" Katie has so many questions. I want Roman to be on his way. I want to get the bags in, get Dexter out for a walk, get settled.

Roman laughs. It's a low, deep booming sound, and Dexter growls and ducks behind my leg.

"Hey," I say. "Hey, it's okay."

Roman only laughs more.

"Live in the woods? Do I live in the woods?" He keeps laughing, as though that is an answer, and he rests his hand on Katie's shoulder.

"She's a good one," he says, turning to me. "You two have a great few days here. My number is just there on the notice board. Everything you need is in that folder, and when you leave, just pop the keys through the letterbox."

"You have a spare too?" I ask. It seems obvious that he would, and I don't know why I even bother to say it.

"Of course, of course. Hopefully you won't lock yourselves out, but yes, yes. Any problems, you call me."

"Sure," I say. I try to keep my tone friendly and upbeat, but I want him gone.

I pick up the folder that he pointed towards, and turn my attention to it, leafing through the clear plastic pockets filled with takeaway menus, Wi-Fi code, instructions on how to use the Aga.

He takes the hint, nods to each of us, and heads for the door.

He reaches out to the handle, then turns back. "Anything at all. Call me."

"Thank you, Mr Blackheath," Katie says. Her voice is saccharine-sweet, but he laps it up, smiles and leaves.

As soon as he is out of the building, I bend down to Dexter and unclip the lead from his collar.

"There you go, boy. There you go."

Katie makes an excited squeaking noise, like a happy little mouse, and flings her arms around me.

"This place!" she squeals. "It's amazing! Didn't I do well? Didn't I?" She bobs up and down, moving me with her.

"You did well, Pie."

I bend down and kiss her dark curls. She smells sweet, or rather she smells like sweets. Fruity, sugary. I want to gag. Instead, I breathe her in, inhaling deep into my lungs. This could be what we needed. This could be something good. I've been an asshole, I really have. I know. I've got to try harder. I've got to start trying.

She squeezes me tightly, with more strength than I would have credited her with.

"I'll make drinks, you go and fetch the bags?" The inflection makes it sound like a question, but really, it's a command.

I nod. "Dexter can come out with me. I'll run him around the house, then fetch the stuff. Okay?"

She puckers her lips into a frown and almost becomes moping, miserable Katie again, but stops just short. She looks at Dexter and saves the moment with a smile.

"Sure. He needs it. I'll run around the place being nosy and excited while you're gone."

I knew already that was exactly what she would do.

"Come on, Dexter." He's at my heel before I finish saying his name.

I open the door, and let Dexter run ahead of me into the dark of the woods.

I know I should probably have given the lad a proper run, but after ten minutes of watching him sniffing at the bottom of every tree we pass, I'm ready to head back to the cabin. Not that I want to get back to Katie, not really. I do want to keep her sweet though, or at least not wind her up. She'll already have gotten bored of snooping. She'll be sitting cross-armed, cross-faced on the sofa by now, internally cursing me, and waiting for me to return so that she can externally curse me. The longer I leave it, the deeper her resentment of my absence will have set in.

I need to snap myself out of this mindset before I go back.

Dexter bobs along next to me. No need to keep him on a lead out here. He's a big dog, sure, but he's better trained than I am. He sticks by my side, cocking his leg at random points to mark the trunks he likes. Tomorrow I'll let Katie have a lie-in and bring Dexter for a long trek.

I can barely see three feet in front of us. I should have thought this through, Blackheath must have a torch in the cabin. Instead, all I have is the shitty light from my phone, and it's not helping much at all.

"Hey, Dexter." His head tilts, and he looks up at me expectantly. "Want to go back to see Katie?" His expression doesn't change. Seems he's as indifferent as I am. "Want to go get your dinner?" Of course, he is much more interested in this idea.

His heavy tail thrashes wildly and he presses his wet nose into my hand, knocking my glowing phone to the leaf-mulch ground.

"Hey! Hey, chill!"

I give him a smile and bend to pick my phone back up. At least the path is soft, there's no danger of me breaking it. My head is level with Dexter's as I squat on the track wiping off a wet leaf, a piece of damp bark and a thick blob of mud. Dexter suddenly lets out a low, deep growl, right into my ear.

He's looking off to our left, further into the woodland. I can't see anything.

"What? What is it?" I whisper, keeping my voice calm. I don't want him getting worked up now, I want him settled, ready for a night in front of the fire, snoozing while Katie and I, well, you know.

He answers me with another long, tremulous growl.

"Dexter." I don't know whether to stand up, see if I can see what it is that's raising his hackles, or to stay down and hope that he scares off whatever it is. If there's anything there. It could be nothing. It's probably nothing.

Then I hear something. Nothing concrete. Movement, like something pushing through something leafy, through bushes, between trees, I don't know. I can only hear the rustling sound. It could be anything. A deer? A badger? I'm sure of one thing – it's not a bear. Whatever it is, Dexter doesn't like it.

"Let's go back," I say into his soft, alert ear. "Let's go, boy."

Dexter looks at me, looks towards the direction of the rustling, and looks back at me again.

"Let's go get your dinner. Come on."

I take one more look into the darkness in the direction of the sound, as Dexter tugs me in the direction of the cabin. We're not used to being out here, out of town. We usually get a run around the block or a lap of the park. The normal noises of nature are bound to make Dex prick up his ears.

I decide not to mention the sound to Katie. What's the point in getting her on edge too? Dex will settle down as soon as he gets his food; Katie would fret all night. That's not why we are here. That's the opposite of why we are here. Instead, I smile and kiss her.

She pulls back and looks at me as though I am forgetting something. I know I must have done something wrong (already) and my mind races quickly through the possibilities.

"Get the bags, Bun Bun," she squeaks.

Of course. How could I be so stupid.

"Sure." I bend to kiss her again, and turn, my face snapping into a grimace as soon as it's out of her view.

We are only staying for five days, but Katie has managed to bring two suitcases and a travel bag. They are only small cases, but really? I have my gym bag and a spare pair of walking shoes. I'm not into fashion, but my trainers were expensive, and I don't plan on traipsing them through the woods every day. I would have changed before taking Dexter out if I hadn't been so desperate to get out there.

I'm one of those stereotypical poker players who lives in jeans and hoodies. I've got a World Series T-shirt that Katie bought me as a Christmas present, but I'm not bankrolled to actually play the tournaments there. I've never even been to Vegas, but every time Katie brings up marriage I suggest that we should plan a visit to the Little Chapel and be joined in matrimony by an Elvis impersonator. I know she won't do it, so it's an easy get out for me.

She always said we should do it while her mother could still attend. Too late for that now, so there's no rush anymore. I can't believe I'm still even thinking about that considering why we are here. This is more Last Chance Saloon than wedding bells at the Little Chapel.

I throw my sports bag over my left shoulder and her travel bag over my right and lift the suitcases. Katie is standing in the doorway, the warm light from the cabin framing her curvy body.

I'm not allowed to use that word if I am speaking to her – curvy. Apparently it has negative connotations. ("You think I'm fat." "I didn't say that." "Curvy. It means fat." Cue three-hour argument.) Personally, I like it. I like her curves.

She could come over to help me carry all this shit in, but both she and Dexter are standing, watching me, as if the threshold of the cabin is some kind of magic forcefield that they aren't allowed to cross over.

I get back inside and set the cases down onto the floor. I'm about to unsling the bags from my shoulders when I catch Katie's expression.

"What?"

"Are you expecting me to take them into the bedroom?" Her voice has slipped back into that thin whine.

I stand for a beat, looking at her. In a way, it's like playing a hand of poker. I know that if I make the wrong move now, I'm likely to lose. There's no point insisting that she moves them. There's no point explaining that I want to crash on the sofa and I don't give a toss about the bags right now.

I smile and pick the cases back up.

Her tone changes in a snap. "Let me show you the bedroom."

She jumps ahead of me, all kitten-playful, soft and faux-adorable. I keep my smile fixed and nod my head for her to continue.

I follow her through the kitchen and down a tight corridor into the bedroom. The wide, soft-looking bed is the centrepiece in terms of floorspace, but my eye carries up past it to a taxidermized stag head mounted proudly on the wall above it. The light from the warm vanilla bulb glints off its eyes, animating it in a way that makes me feel instantly uneasy.

"Nice cliché," I say, as I put Katie's cases down next to the bed. I drop her bag on top and put my own bag onto the bed.

"I kind of like him. If you're going to come to a cabin in the woods, you need a stuffed deer head. I would have felt cheated without one." She jumps up onto the bed and stands eye-to-eye with the dead animal.

"Yeah, okay."

Katie turns around and lets her body drop down into the thick softness of the duvet.

I want a beer, some food, and maybe a shower, but I can see already what she wants.

She pats the bed next to her and gives my bag a swift shove so that it lands on the floor with a heavy THUCK. The sound of the impact triggers a thought of the badger. With that, and the dead stag giving me the evil eye, I am hardly in the mood for what Katie has in mind.

I'm still wearing my jacket; I haven't even had time to take that off yet. I tug at my sleeves and throw it up over the stag's head. See no evil.

Katie stretches her legs, expanding her body to fill the bed space.

"It's so comfortable," she says. "Come and try it."

I never know with Katie whether she wants me because she wants to be in control, and she thinks that this is how to achieve it, or whether she actually wants *me*. That smile could be real, or it could be a weapon.

I'm stalling; I recognise it, and the pause starts to feel uncomfortable.

She reaches up and unclips the barrette that's been keeping her hair under control all day. Her black curls fall around her pretty, pale face and drop onto her shoulders. It gets me every time. I don't know, there's just something about the way that it makes her look so innocent, but so amazingly sexy at the same time.

She knows, of course. She knows what she's doing. She knows me, and I know her. Here we are, so familiar with each other, so aware of each other's moves. I still don't know how the hand is going to play out. I still don't know if the odds are stacked too heavily against us, or if there's a chance we could come out of this on top.

Chapter Four

Next morning, I leave Katie sleeping. Most days she'd be awake before me, and if she wasn't then Dexter would be, and he'd be hoofing into the bedroom, waking us both up anyway. The excitement of the journey must have knocked his body rhythm off kilter, as there's no sign of him yet.

The clock says that it's only seven thirty, but I slept solidly after Katie and I finished. I probably fell asleep before she was ready for me to, but I did my bit, I played my part. Sometimes I feel my age. I mean I'm only five years older than her, but I'm heading for forty and she's only just tipped into her thirties, there's quite a difference I suppose. I can handle late nights, but only as long as I catch up on sleep the next day. Katie works shifts; she can sleep on a knife-edge. Anytime, anywhere, she can close her eyes, lie quietly for ten minutes and she's away. I guess I did just the same last night. She can't have been that pissed off with me though, because she let me sleep. Either I did a good job of making her happy or I had disappointed her enough for one day. Who knows?

I slip out of bed as quietly as possible and tread softly on the bare wooden floor. My feet are slightly moist from the warmth of the bed and they make a tiny sucker-like sound as I walk. I should have unpacked last night, because I'm sure that searching through my bag for something to wear is either going to awaken Katie or make Dex come running in here and do the job. I pull out the first T-shirt I find, grab a pair of clean pants, and put them on with yesterday's jeans. I almost go for the socks that I threw under the chair last night but think better of it. Make an effort. Try to make an effort, Seb.

Before I duck into the bathroom, I head through to the kitchen and find Dex's basket empty. He's up already? So, where has he gone?

"Dex?" I say, hoping that I've struck the right balance between him hearing me and Katie not being woken up by my voice. "Dexter?"

Nothing.

I don't have to look far to find him. He's found his way back into the living area and snuggled into the rug. It's made of a thick, long beige-coloured fur, and although I believe that it's probably the real deal, I can't put my finger on what kind of animal it might come from.

"Hey Dex," I say gently into his ear. "Hey boy."

He opens one eye and looks at me, then sticks out his tongue to lick my hand.

"Still sleepy?" I say and he slowly, casually wags his tail.

I'm surprised at how awake I feel, considering. I think that subconsciously I'm aware that this is the only time I will have alone, without Katie, while we are here. Early mornings, if she is still asleep. Now I'm consciously aware of it too, and that makes me even more determined not to wake her, and to spend my time wisely.

Despite the cabin being as far away from a casino as she could find, I was actually quite pleased with her choice of location. I much prefer this to some foreign tourist-filled beach or a high-rise city break. Poker aside, if anyone had asked me what kind of getaway I'd like, I would probably have chosen something very much like this. It's kind of like those holiday parks that cost the world and have you spending just as much having a hawk fly onto your hand or sharing a swimming pool with three hundred screaming kids, but…well, without the kids and without the expense. I wouldn't be surprised if there are hawks though, even if they are not quite as well trained here.

"I'm going to brush my teeth and then I'll come back to you boy, okay?" I ask, even though I know he has no idea what I'm saying. I'm careful not to say the 'w-a-l-k' word yet though, once I do, we'll be committed to leaving right then, and my mouth tastes like…well, it tastes like I fell asleep without brushing my teeth last night.

The bathroom has a ceiling skylight, but the sun is only just starting to illuminate the day. It's a pleasant kind of dimness that is sufficient for me to clean my teeth and splash water on my face without me having to see too much detail of what I look like. My comb is still in my bag, so I pick up a huge bristle brush that Katie has left on the little shelf in front of the mirror and pull that through my hair. The static causes my dark mop to fly in all directions. I put the brush down and give up.

I could use a coffee, but the kitchen is next to the bedroom and I don't want to risk it until Dex and I have had our walk. When I get back, I'll make coffee, make breakfast, make Katie happy, but for now, I want to get out of here while I still can.

I get back to the kitchen and Dex has his nose in his water bowl, splashing the contents over the slate-tiled floor, pushing the metal container so it makes a muffled scuffling sound. I wince at the noise, but I can hardly stop him from drinking. I take a glass from the cupboard, pour myself a drink from the tap too, and then pause just before I knock it back. There's something in there. Okay, I should have checked first, or at least I should have rinsed it before using it. Who knows how long this place was empty before we got here? I mean it's a great place, so maybe it's booked out back-to-back, week after week, but maybe no one has been here for months. Who knows? I throw the contents into the white porcelain Belfast sink, and there it is, a little dried up, scrunched spider. I say little. I don't expect it was quite so little when it was alive, patrolling this place. Its legs are curled up to its body, and its body is the size of a juicy raisin. I guess it wouldn't have tasted like that. It turns my stomach. I can feel a flush of nausea, I turn on the tap and sluice it away before that feeling overwhelms me. I can't use that glass now. I put my mouth below the flowing water and take a few long, clean gulps. Dexter has finished what he was doing, and he's run over to the door, standing there expectantly, knowing what comes next.

"Okay," I say. "Okay, Dex."

I throw on my jacket and pick up his lead. For a second, I pause, wondering whether to attach it to his lead, but I decide against it.

The sky is a pale silver-grey, and the morning light has turned the trees into dark silhouettes. I inhale deeply, taking in the clear, clean air. We don't exactly live in the city, but here, everything feels somehow more fresh, more free. Dexter bounds off towards the edge of the woods again, exactly the same way he directed us last night. Sure. If he likes it that way, let's go again. We have all week to try out the other tracks.

The leaves on the woodland floor are damp, but the twigs still snap with a dry click as I walk over them. Dex is keeping to the path. It's a thin, weedy line, made by people who have trodden this way before rather than being an official walkway. There's no gravel track or National Trust-ordained pedestrianism here. Verdant branches hang low across my chest, which makes me think that not many people come down here – or at least not recently. It's Blackheath's land though, all of it, so maybe he just doesn't like visitors. Maybe he doesn't encourage visitors. Either way, it suits me, and by the way that Dexter is galloping ahead, enjoying his off-lead freedom, it clearly suits him too.

We've made it three hundred yards into the woods before I realise that I left my phone back in the cabin. I was only going to check the time. I'm not really one of those people who constantly checks their social media, taking photos of the world to share on Instasnap or whatever; I leave all that to Katie. You can be sure that while I was out here last night with Dex she would have been photographing the cabin from every angle, running the shots through countless filters, and uploading to every account she has. Personally, I like to live in the moment, and experience things for what they are rather than how many likes I can get for sharing them. With Katie still sleeping, and no one else that I need to contact, not having my phone with me is a minor issue. If Katie wakes up and gets pissy with me for not being contactable, then, well, whatever.

Out here, there's a heavy stench of deep, earthy scents. Damp woodland, mixed up with the fragrance of everything green that has fallen to the floor and started to rot. You'd think that might be an unpleasant aroma, but somehow, it's not. It isn't the scent of composting, it's something else, something natural. Perhaps it's the smell of nature itself. It's delicious. If the colour of dark green had an aroma, this would be it.

The path is overgrown, and my boots are soaked already. I can see Dexter bobbing along up ahead, a little dark shape in the distance.

"Slow up, Dex. Hey."

He stops, turns his head, and whips his tail from side to side.

If nothing else comes of this week, at least Dexter is having a great time. I trot along to catch up with him.

I haven't set my hopes too high. I mean, I want things to work with Katie, I really do, but I feel like whatever I do, it's never going to be enough for her.

When did it get like this? Were we always a mismatch and I just didn't see it?

No. Not at all. We were happy. Strangely, we were the happiest when I was my unhappiest. She was still working at the Coffee Express, I was still a slave to Vesper UK, the energy-sapping, soul-destroying sales company. I get a heavy sick feeling in my gut every time I think of that place. We were screwing people over, and I knew it. Trawling through data, picking out the people that we thought were the biggest suckers, so we could sell them things they didn't need at a price they couldn't afford. It's a lot easier than you'd think, and that makes it even sicker.

Before I met Katie, I would work all day, and play poker every night. Poker was my escape. It was a hobby. It was fun. I miss those days. The game changes when you're playing for money that you need to make a living, when you're playing to pay your bills and put food on the table. Someone once said it's a hard way to make an easy living, and they were right.

Still, Katie and I liked the same kind of music, the same films, the same restaurants. We went out, we stayed in, mainly at my place. Her flatmate back then was a rather intolerant prissy girl who'd probably never had a boyfriend of her own, if that's what she was into. She didn't like having me round. It didn't matter. I was happy to have Katie in my flat, to myself, to be as loud as we wanted to be, and back then, we were loud. Back then we were crazy.

After I met Katie, I had to cut down on my poker nights. Not straight away of course. We weren't all that serious to begin with, just like most people. I wasn't looking for a relationship, and she seemed happy enough carrying on with her life, hanging out with her female friends, going to the gym, all that sort of stuff. She had her time, I had mine, and then we had time together. It was perfect.

The closer we got, the more we ate into each other's lives. The me-time diminished for both of us. My poker nights went from six nights-a-week to four, and then to two. Even that seemed too much for her. I was working, seeing Katie, eating, and sleeping. That was it. I thought it was the work that was getting me down. I'm sure it was. It was work that was making me unhappy.

"If you don't like it, quit," Katie told me.

Simple. She made it sound so simple.

I was thirty-one. I felt like I was getting old, like I'd done nothing with my life, nothing that I wanted to do anyway.

"Don't keep doing something that's making you miserable."

What else could I do? What skills did I have?

Katie was still cranking out the lattes at Coffee Express, but I could tell she wasn't happy either.

"Take your own advice," I said.

And she did.

Within the week she had handed in her notice and signed on with an agency doing care work.

Whether she was calling my bluff or just needed that push to make the change, she jumped ahead, she moved on, she did what I wasn't doing. She dropped everything and changed her life.

Once she moved to shift work, I could start playing poker more often again. I had free nights in the week after she set out to the home. I could either lounge around the flat in my pants, because yes, we had moved in together by then, or I could get it together and go back to what I loved even more than my laziness.

I went back to the casino. The game had changed. There were more recreational players, people who weren't so good at the game but liked to play for fun. The ideal opponents. Rich old men, foreign students, dumb women, all out to have a good evening playing cards rather than necessarily making a profit. Of course, there were a couple of guys who knew what they were doing, but as long as I stayed away from big clashes with them, well, I could clean up.

Two months later, and eight grand up, I decided, yes, fuck it, time to commit. I quit my day job and took the plunge.

"That's not really what I had in mind," Katie told me, never trying to hide her disappointment in me. For the first time in a long time though, I felt free. I felt in control of my own life again. I felt happy.

I got to see Katie during the day when she wasn't on shift, which was an improvement on when I was at Vesper, but that didn't seem to matter to her. I knew she was displeased with my decision.

During the good months when I'm winning and bringing home three, four times what I would have made in sales, she's happy. When I run bad and have a losing month, she barely speaks to me. There's constant tension in our lives, and I know that a large part of that is down to what I do. I blame myself. I blame poker. But I'm not going to give it up. I love her, but she pushed me into making this choice. Without her, I would probably never have left my job and gone pro. She created the monster that I am, and now she's got to put up with it.

We were happy though. I remember. We were happy. We could be again.

I catch up with Dex. He's stopped to dig at something by the side of the track. There's a small heap of earth, stacked neatly into a pile and he's got his nose down into it. He must smell the mole, down there, somewhere below.

"Get off, come on," I say, giving him the tiniest tap with my boot on his rear end.

He doesn't look up.

"Hey. Dex. Come on."

He's shifting his head from left to right, trying to get in there. Mole has got to be near the surface to wind him up this much.

I crouch by his side, slip my hand into his collar, and I'm about to lift his head back when I notice it.

There's a thick band on the ground, running beside the molehill, and on over the path. Without getting up I can see that it leads off into the undergrowth on either side of the track, in one long, unbroken line. I put my fingers down into it. It's soft, powdery, like fine sand. No, more like grey ash. The band is about four inches wide. How far does it run? As far as I can see that's for sure. A niggling thought hits me as I let the powder fall to the ground: I've seen this before somewhere, but where?

I meant to stick to the path, carry on ahead for our jaunt this morning, explore what's out in Blackheath's land, but now curiosity is getting the better of me. I want to head off-track, follow the line, see where it goes, maybe find out why it's here. Why. Does there have to be a why? Most things have a reason, and if they don't, humans have a cute way of driving themselves nuts trying to work one out anyway. I do. I know I do.

Dexter's making frantic panting noises as he tried to burrow into the mole hole.

"Leave it, let's go," I say, and gently pull his head up. "Come on. You want to go into the woods?"

I figure that all he knows is that he wants to go for a walk, and whichever direction I head, he will follow. More likely, if I set off into the woodland, he will soon run ahead, and I'll be the one following.

I reach into my back pocket and remember that I left my phone back at the cabin. I don't have time to go too far right now. I want to be back before Katie wakes up, wonders where I am, and starts having a hissy fit that I'm not there. I take a final look at the dirt, then ruffle the fur on Dex's head.

Okay. Fine. We can come out again later.

"Let's get back to Katie." He puts his head back down towards the ground. "Let's go get your breakfast."

That gets his attention. He wags his heavy black tail and gets ready to set off back the way we came.

I'll check out the line next time I bring Dex for a walk, when I've told Katie where I'm going. I won't tell her what I'm going for. If I tell her that I'm going to investigate some line in the ground, she'll give me that look. The one that she gives me when she wants me to grow up and start acting my age rather than playing around like a teenager. Sometimes I like playing around like a teenager. I like a bit of adventure. I like feeling free.

Dex thunders off in the direction of the cabin, and I follow, ever the good boy.

I needn't have worried. When we get back, despite Dexter slamming his bowl into the bottom of the kitchen cabinet as soon as I've filled it for him, Katie is soundly asleep. I pick up my phone and see it's eight forty-five. We were out longer than I thought. Still, it makes little difference, seeing as she's still flat out.

I perch next to her and scroll through my phone. I check the news, nothing exciting has happened, and flick through my emails. Back when I was in sales, I would have received ten, fifteen messages through to my Blackberry by now, even when I was meant to be on holiday. There was never any let up. Evenings, weekends, whenever the boss needed me, I was meant to answer. Now the only messages I get are the spam marketing mails that go straight through to my junk folder, and updates from the poker mailing lists that I'm signed up to. Not very interesting for anyone other than me. I don't want to think about playing while I'm here and not able to, so I click my phone closed and put it down on the table next to the bed.

Katie's long black hair is swirled around her head like a silk scarf. I want to reach over and stroke through the curls, but I don't want to wake her. I can just see her pale nose and the trace of her top lip, plump and ripe. She's beautiful when she is sleeping. Silence suits her. I'm just about to lean over and brush the hair from her face, to kiss her soft pink cheek, when Dexter comes bouncing in.

I haven't made breakfast yet. I was going to get it together, brew the coffee, toast some bread, make it look like I was making an effort. Instead, here I am, sitting on the side of the bed with cold, empty hands. It's too late though. Dex leaps onto the bed and Katie is awake.

She lets out a muffled groan and bats her hand feebly in Dexter's direction.

He lies next to her, pressing himself as closely as he can to her body.

"Dex, no," I say, and point to the floor. "Get off. Get down."

He pretends he's not looking at me and wags his tail slowly.

"It's okay," Katie says quietly into the pillow. "What time is it?"

"Nearly nine," I say. "Sleep alright?"

"Yeah."

She rolls onto her back and the duvet slips just enough for me to see the creamy curve of her breast. She notices my stare and tugs the cover over herself.

"Stop that."

Her tone is coy and light; I've not annoyed her yet today.

"I was going to make you breakfast," I say. "Do you want to stay here with Dex, and I'll bring you something?"

"What are you after?" she asks. "You must want something to be being this nice to me."

"I want you, Pie." I stroke her curls away from the side of her face. "I want to make everything good between us again. That's why I am here with you." I don't want to argue. I don't want us shouting at each other every day. I don't want to fight anymore. "I was thinking about it while

I was out with Dexter. I want us to be happy. I know we can be." At least I am being honest.

She gives me a slight look of doubt, but quickly covers it up. One skill I have honed from playing poker is my ability to read when people are bluffing me. I don't always get it right, but Katie is very easy to read.

"I want that too," she says. I'm not convinced that she believes it is going to work, but I'm not convinced that I believe it either. There are more reasons to be together than to be apart though, so in poker terms the odds are in our favour.

My hand is still on her hair. I'm leaning over her, my breath fresh, hers stale from sleep, mixing together in the space between us. The moment hangs. I could get back into bed with her, make love again like we did last night or…

Dex jumps to his feet, instantly alert. He stands, tense from nose to tail, staring out of the window. There's no bark yet, but his body is brewing up a low grumbling growl.

"What? What is it? Someone out there?" I ask him.

Katie shuffles up the bed into a sitting position, trying to pull the duvet with her to cover her naked body, but Dexter is still standing on it, and as she tugs it slowly, he stumbles.

He's soon back on his feet, and back into exactly the same position, staring out at something that I still can't see.

I get up and walk over to the window. The world looks brighter than it did an hour ago when we first went out. The sun is making the leaves lighter, more vivid. It's certainly a beautiful view, but I can't see anything out of the ordinary.

Dexter breaks into a full-voiced bark, and jumps forward a little on the bed, as if snapping at something.

"Dex," I say, turning back to look at him.

Katie shrugs. "I'll make the breakfast. Why don't you go and see what's spooking him?"

Sure. Like I want to find whatever's upsetting him.

"What am I meant to do if it's a…" I search my brain for a list of potentially dangerous animals that could possibly be a threat to any of us, and I come up blank. No bears. No wolves. Okay, maybe it's fine. "Yeah. Thanks," I say, and bend to kiss her.

"Come on boy," I say to Dex, but he doesn't move. "Dexter. Let's go get it."

Still, he stands on the bed, his body rumbling with the growl that passes like a low hum from his snarling mouth.

"I guess I'll go on my own then."

I pull my boots back on and click the latch on the door. As I turn to wave to Katie, I see her get out of bed, slipping her legs to the side and standing naked and beautiful. I'd rather not be going outside. I'd rather be getting back into bed with her, getting back into her, doing what it was we came here for. I don't think that our relationship can be fixed by sex, but it certainly won't harm it.

Dex is still standing on the bed, but he hears the door as I pull it open and looks back towards me.

"Coming?" I ask him. He looks towards the window once more, and then galumphs off the bed, onto the floor and races to my side. "Good lad."

Katie slips on some pants and a vest, and Dexter and I go back outside into the cold morning once more.

I let him guide me, as we head in the general direction that he was barking at.

Probably saw a bird or a deer riffled the trees or something. I'm sure it can't be much else. He's not used to this environment, being amidst nature, having all these unusual (to him) animals and plants around. Best to get him settled, let him see there's nothing to be scared of.

"Okay boy? Nothing here, see. Nothing here."

I don't see anything, but he's still on alert. His fur is puffed, on end, and his teeth are still bared. He's holding his tail high, making himself big and bold and fearsome, or as fearsome as he can be. He looks at me and walks ahead, off the path and into the wood.

"Hey. Wait." He's speeding up, jumping over muddy patches that look like they have recently been puddles, skipping over low branches, winding between bushes. "Dex!"

I try to keep up, but he's changing direction, heading further into the woodland, as if he knows where he is going, as if he has been here before. I speed my pace, feel my breath straining as I break into a jog. I'm unfit, I know it. I have a gym membership, sure, but I've been three times in the two years that I've been a member. It's a twenty-four-hour centre, on the same road as the casino, I thought it would be ideal for my schedule, but it only serves to provide more hours in the day that I can avoid going. My only exercise is walking Dex, and I am a few pounds over my ideal weight. By a few pounds I mean about a stone. It's never usually an issue, but now, trying to make my legs maintain this run, and trying to make my body obey my demands, I'm struggling almost as soon as I've begun.

"Dex! Dexter!" I can't see him. I run on, and come to a fallen tree, its trunk standing to my waist, even on its side. It must have grown here for centuries until it fell. It blocks my path, and before I continue, I stop, resting my hands against it, taking a few deep breaths. I can hear Dexter barking. Once, twice, and then again and again. He's found something, I can tell. I can also tell which direction he is in.

These boots were not designed for running. My left ankle is chafing against the inside of the hard leather. I bend down to rub it, and there it is again, a thick heavy line of grey powder. It's exactly the same as the line I found earlier. I do a quick calculation of my position. Could it be the same line? A continuation? It's possible.

My thoughts are stopped dead when Dexter's barking is replaced by a blood-curdling yelp. It's the kind of noise I have only heard from him when Katie accidentally stepped on his paw once. It's like that, only far worse.

Shit.

"Dexter!" I rub my ankle, stand up, and run, run in the direction of the sound of him, run towards whatever has hurt him, unafraid, thinking only of helping my dog. "Dexter!" I shout again.

He's silent now. No barking, no yelping, nothing to guide me, but I have a good sense of direction and a good idea of where he is.

"I'm coming boy. Where are you?" I hope that by shouting I will scare off whatever it is that has harmed him. Maybe he just fell, I tell myself, but I don't believe it. I don't think he stepped on something or stumble-tripped. I think something hurt him, and I need to get to him now.

As I get closer to the place that I thought I heard him, there's a soft whimpering that I know is Dex.

"Hey," I say. "Hey, I'm here, it's okay." My voice is soft now, but I'm scouring the spaces between the trees, looking for movement between the bushes, trying to pick up any trace of danger that I can perceive. I want Dex to stay calm, but I am finding it hard to calm myself, not knowing what might be out there.

I see him, lying on the ground, between two bushes. He's on his side, and his body is rising and falling rapidly with his breaths. He's hyperventilating. He hears me and lifts his head, letting out a soft groaning whimper.

"Dex. Ssh. It's okay." I keep saying it, but I don't really believe it's true. I crouch next to him, keeping my head up, while I look all around us, trying to pick up on any danger before I turn my gaze down to my brave boy.

Did he find whatever it was that he was chasing? Is that what did this? Still, I am not imaginative enough to think of a wild animal that would bring Dex to the ground like this. I run my hand over him, and then I see it. It's his rear leg, the left one. He's holding it up towards himself, bringing it in to his body. There's something hard, dull, metallic around his ankle, and something red, sticky and hot that can only be one thing. He's bleeding. I recoil my hand and look him in the eyes.

"You okay boy? You're okay. You're going to be okay."

I reach down, back to his leg, but just as I am about to investigate further, I hear a loud cracking noise from the treeline.

I put my finger on my lips, telling Dex to hush his growl, not to bark. "Ssh. Easy, Dex."

I slowly move my head, trying to remain unseen, but trying to pick out what made the noise. Again. Further to our right, slightly deeper into the wood, another noise. A smaller snap, and then rustling. Something moving away, back into the trees. Good. It's not coming towards us then. Good.

Dexter can't control his noise any longer and he lets out a pained bark.

Immediately I hear a scuffling rushed movement sound from the direction of the previous crack-snaps. I see something. I think I see something. The light is dim out here and crouched between the bushes it's hard to be sure of anything at all, but I'm sure for a moment that I see something. It looks like the shape of a person. Around the right size, but there's only a flash of movement, merely the slightest glimpse, and then – gone. I look down at Dex. I can't go chasing off into the woods after whoever it might have been, I have to find out what has happened to him, sort it out, get him back to the cabin.

"Is someone there?" I shout. "I see you. I see you. You'd better keep the fuck away from me and keep the fuck away from my dog."

There's no reply. I didn't expect there would be, but I had to say it, I had to fire a warning shot.

I wait, five seconds, ten, and see and hear nothing more. All the time I run my hand over Dex's head, calming, reassuring.

When I am sure that we are alone, or at least as sure as I can be, I look back at his bloody leg.

It's wire. There's a wire loop around his leg, like some kind of snare. I've never encountered anything like this in real life, but I've read enough adventure books to know it's probably been laid here to catch rabbits. An accident then? He stumbled into this while he was chasing after whoever that was? Who knows? It looks that way.

The wire is digging into his flesh. I pull at the loop, trying to loosen the noose from around his fur. It slides, releasing him, and he bends his head to lick at the wounded area. The blood isn't gushing from him, it looks, from what I can see in the dull light, to be superficial.

"That's it. That's better. Yes, you're okay." I stroke his head as he licks himself clean.

I pick up the loop of wire and turn it over in my hands. It's attached to a wooden stick that was no doubt stuck into the ground before Dex pulled it loose, trying to free himself from the trap. We're going to have to be careful out here. Stick to the path or watch out for shit like this. I guess it's normal in the woods, on private land, to come across things like rabbit traps. We are lucky that there are no bears, and that there are no bear traps. He might have lost a leg like that, never mind got a scratch on his leg. It's more than a scratch, I know, I can see it, but compared to what could have happened it's pretty mild.

"Can you walk? You going to be able to walk back?"

We've come further than we did on our walk earlier. I don't know how far we are from the cabin, but I hope I don't have to carry him. I take my hand from his head, and get to my feet, hoping that he will follow my lead and do the same.

He gingerly stutters to a standing position. There's a pained look on his face, but he's up and on all four legs.

"Good lad. Well done. Can you walk?"

I move a few steps away from him and stop.

He looks at me, and then slowly makes his way over. His back leg cringes a little, and he's obviously not putting all his weight onto it as he hobbles, unbalanced towards me.

"That's it." I pat him softly.

Katie will be wondering where we are, but I see little point in texting her. If I tell her what has happened, she will only worry more. Hopefully she is keeping busy, making breakfast, checking her morning Instagram feed and not bothering too much about what's keeping us.

I take a few steps back towards the direction of the path, and pause again, waiting to see if Dexter is able to follow. He's slow, but he's mobile.

"Good boy," I say.

I look back towards where I thought I saw the shape of the person, but there's nothing to be seen now. Maybe Blackheath's family or someone who works for him. Who knows? He never warned us about not wandering off path, out into the woods, and he never told us that we couldn't come out here. Perhaps he's used to his guests staying in the cabin and using it as a love nest, rather than exploring his grounds. It probably never even dawned on him that someone would want to be an adventurer out here. Perhaps it should have.

I ruffle Dex's thick black fur once more before we turn and walk back to track, and back down it to the cabin.

"Why didn't you message me? What's that? Where's that blood from?"

The questions come thick and fast when we get back to Katie. She sees me, then the snare, and finally Dex, trailing blood onto the slate floor. Only a little. It seems to be on his paws, as he leaves behind a dirty red-black trail.

"Keep him out of the bedroom," she adds, quickly.

Sure. We don't want our dog to bleed onto our bedcovers, or onto our clothes. What an inconvenience that would be.

"Sure," I say, keeping the rest of my thoughts to myself. "He got caught in a snare. It was an accident. Looks okay though." I squat down on the tiles next to him and take a proper look in the light of the kitchen. There's just a thin red line, a little jagged, like an angry bracelet around his ankle.

"You should clean that," Katie says. She's already reaching into the cupboard for a bowl, running warm water from the tap, and placing it on the floor next to me and Dex. "Cotton wool," she says, half to me and half to herself, as she wanders up to the bedroom to raid her make-up bag. She comes back with a handful of rabbit-tail balls, white and fluffy, and drops them into the bowl.

I squeeze water from one of the cotton wool lumps and wipe at Dex's leg. He yelps immediately.

"Gently!" Katie barks.

"Do you want to do it?" I say, more harshly than I had intended.

"Okay," she says, taking over the role happily, seemingly not noticing the barb in my voice. She loves this kind of thing. I think that's why she enjoys working in the care home. She gets such a kick out of doing things for those led fortunate than herself. Perhaps that's why she still likes being with me, despite everything. She gets to help someone who is less able than herself. Less able? Less fortunate? Less? Probably that. Probably sees me as inferior and in need of help. I'm not even sure that she is wrong.

Dex lies still and lets her dab the wet cotton wool onto his wound. She does a good job, he doesn't complain and soon there are five slightly blood-tarnished balls sitting on the floor next to the bowl, and Dex's leg looks clean.

"It's not bleeding now," Katie says. "It looks like a scratch to his skin, nothing more. Doesn't seem to have gone deep at all. You must have got to him before he could struggle and hurt himself more."

I guess he was clever enough to know not to thrash about and pull the snare tighter around himself. Or maybe he did move, notice the difference as the noose tightened and realised he had to stop. Dogs must be smarter than rabbits.

He has gone back to licking the wound, and I leave him to it, as Katie stands up, picks up the bowl and the used balls, and tidies up behind herself.

"He should be fine," she says. "I can't believe that guy Roman didn't warn us though.

I shrug. "Why would he? Probably didn't expect us to be off the track on his land."

"You were off the track? Did you find something then? You worked out what it was he was barking at?"

I pause.

"No. I mean yes. We were off the track. I thought he was chasing something, but…no, I didn't see anything. Before he caught up with whatever it was, this happened." I wave at the snare that I've put down on the worktop.

"You didn't need to bring that dirty thing home with you," she says.

"I didn't want to leave it out there to hurt anything again."

"Whoever put it there must have more of these," she picks it up, examines it, pokes her finger into the small loop. "They won't be happy with you for stopping them catching their dinner, I'm sure."

"People don't live off the rabbits they catch for dinner, Pie. We are in Wessex, not the Middle Ages."

She shrugs, like it's all the same to her. Not the brightest button in the box, but she's a cutie.

She seems happy with my explanation anyway, because she opens up the oven and pulls out exactly what I had been hoping for. A pile of bacon sandwiches that she has been keeping warm. Okay the bread has gotten a bit hard, but the bacon is still piping hot and the butter has melted deliciously into the sourdough.

"You are the best." I grin and scoop my arms around her to hug her and give her a kiss.

"Wash your hands!" she shrieks before I get chance to make contact.

I look at them. Filthy, bloody and disgusting. Nice.

"Give one to Dex," I say, as I scrub my hands under the kitchen tap. "Might cheer him up."

He wags his tail slowly, making a thuck thuck sound against the slate floor. He understands everything we say, I'm sure of it.

After tea and most of the bacon sandwiches, we sit opposite each other at the small wooden table. Dex is back on the rug in front of the empty fireplace, his sore leg curled up beneath him defensively. Not a particularly good start to the week for him, but Katie and I are on good form. No arguments, some sex, and she's not asked me to take her home yet. Feels like I'm winning.

Chapter Five

Emboldened by the lack of conflict between us, I propose a change of scene.

"Do you fancy going out for a drink? There was that pub, back down in the village we came through."

She shrugs.

"What?" I say.

"Only one of us will be able to drink. We'll have to leave Dex at home. Seems like a lot of hassle for a few glasses of wine…and we have bottles in the fridge."

I sigh and run my fingers through my hair, to stop me from clenching my fist.

"We could walk?" I say, as calmly as I can manage. "It's not all that far and you haven't been out today."

"Well, I would have been out if you hadn't let Dexter get injured. It's hardly my fault."

I instinctively open my mouth to reply. I'm about to snap at her, but I manage to catch my words before they tumble out.

"He'll be fine here," I say.

Dexter looks over and sleepily wags his tail. He always knows when to contribute to the conversation.

"We're on holiday. You don't need to get out every day, you can do whatever you want to. I just thought…well, it would be nice to go out while we both have our evenings together." I give her my best smile, and hope that I am looking charming rather than idiotic.

It's her turn to pause now. I can almost hear the words that she was about to say. Our conversations have become so predictable.

"Fine. Whatever." She stands and starts to walk towards the direction of the bedroom, or maybe bathroom, then she calls back to me. "But I'm not walking."

So. I have to drive. At least it gets us out of the cabin for a few hours, and if she is the one who's drinking, maybe she'll be more fun to be around. Seems like a win-win.

"Okay, Pie," I shout after her, but she's ducked into the bathroom and there's no reply.

I feed Dexter and settle him on the rug in front of the closed doors of the wood burner. He gives me a sad look, but I expect he'll be asleep before too long and won't be too upset that we aren't with him. He seems to have settled here more easily than I thought he would. He's stopped limping and fiddling with his hind leg now too, and the sore part has dried and crusted over. I hope I'll be able to take him out again tomorrow. I could definitely go nuts if I'm stuck in here for too long, and I'm almost certain he could too.

Katie is standing at the door waiting for me. She's dressed up for the occasion, far more than necessary, wearing a black dress that sits about two inches above her knees and curves at the neckline to show far too much of her cleavage. On her feet are a pair of spike-heeled ankle boots that I have never seen before. Come to think of it I've not seen her dress before either. She's got her handbag, a black leather postcard-sized thing that I'm sure she can only fit a debit card and a lipstick into, and that's all.

"Not taking a jacket?" I ask, trying to be helpful, but realising as I say it that she's going to think it judgemental.

"I'm not going to be outdoors," she says.

I open my mouth to say that it's going to be difficult for her to get to the car without going outdoors, but I decide better of it.

"Okay, Pie." As an afterthought that should probably have been the first thing I said, I add, "You look great."

"Thanks," she says.

I look as I always look. Jeans, of course, T-shirt, as always, jumper over my T-shirt because it's February in

Wessex not summer in Ibiza. I pick up my jacket from the hook by the door, knowing that I will probably end up lending it to Katie later rather than wearing it myself. Love is a series of small sacrifices.

She almost smiles, until I open the door and the chill of the night hits her like a slap. She says nothing, and she certainly doesn't go to get her coat. She won't back down, Katie, and she won't admit when she's wrong. I want the night to be fun, and I want to avoid an argument, so I follow her lead and say nothing too. Instead, I walk out to the car, open the passenger door for her, and then get into the driver's seat.

She teeters over, her heels rocking on the gravel of the path, and slides in next to me. She's wearing thick stockings at least, or maybe tights. I never can tell until she takes her dress off. Either way, at least she's put a tiny bit of thought into keeping herself warm. I have to stop thinking about it, or my mouth will say something that my brain doesn't want it to.

"He'll be alright, won't he?" she says, clipping in her seatbelt.

"Dex? Sure. He's all snuggled up there. He'll have a great night without us. I'll take him out again in the morning."

"And maybe you can be a bit more careful next time."

I pause and take a breath before responding.

"I'll try, Katie. I'll try."

I flick on the lights and turn the key in the ignition; we head down the road in silence.

I'm lost in my thoughts, focussing on the dark track ahead of me, when the headlights pick out the shape of the badger, or what is left of the badger, lying in our path.

"You made a right mess of him," Katie says, covering her eyes with both hands. I slow the car. "Don't slow down, I don't want to see it. It's disgusting. Bun Bun, please."

She must really mean it if she is resorting to pet names. I'm not actually looking at the pile of grey black white red pink mush though, I'm looking at something else. My mind hadn't picked up on it when I first stopped here. When I crouched at the side of that poor animal, all I could think about was the pain he must have been in. I was focussed completely on the badger. Subconsciously though, I had picked up on the other anomaly. Running next to where the body is smeared across the ground, over the road in front of us and off into the woodland on either side is a four-inch-wide powdery band. In the darkness, illuminated by my headlights, it seems to shine. It looks obvious now in a way it hadn't in the dim evening light of yesterday. The day had only just started to fade then, but now, in the darkness, the line shimmers under the light from the car. I look over at Katie; she is still covering her face, and she doesn't see it.

Tomorrow I'm going to go and follow that line. When I find out what it is, maybe then I will tell her about it.

"Seb! Come ON," she whines.

"Sorry love, I didn't want to run through the…er…stuff," I say, and press the accelerator towards the floor.

There doesn't seem to be any restriction on parking in the village, so I pull up as close as I can to the pub. There are a few streetlights dotted along by the roadside, casting a warm amber glow that makes it feel like a scene from a movie. The pub itself is a whitewashed block of a building, set back slightly from the road to allow the placement of two round picnic tables and attached benches, but these lie empty and their umbrellas are closed and wrapped tight. There's a large bay window, curtains open, and as we pass, heading for the door, I catch the eye of a couple of men playing dominos on the table set into the alcove. They stare back, awkwardly, and I nod and look away as quickly as I feel is polite.

Katie tugs on my sleeve.

"Don't," she says.

I nod. This time she is probably right.

I have to duck to get through the doorway. I'm a flat six feet tall, and I've never had that problem before. For some reason I like it.

In front of an open fire, there's a skinny pale greyhound lying on a threadbare rug. I could open my mouth and point it out to Katie, complain that we could have brought Dex after all, but she wasn't to know. I would have felt like a dick if he had to stay in the car while we were in here drinking slash not drinking. Better that he is in the cabin, warm and safe.

The greyhound lifts his head to look at me, as if he feels my eyes upon him, but more likely he's just picked up the scent of strangers. The other customers can pick it up too. It's not a "everyone turns to look at the out-of-towners" moment, they are more subtle than that, but I can see people glancing at each other, the delicate nod of heads in our direction and furtive peeks.

For a weeknight, it's pretty packed. I figure we are out of luck for seats, and we're going to be standing at the bar, but Katie is Katie, and Katie has no fear, and no particular social grace. To the left of the fireplace, a couple of men, somewhere in their fifties, wearing thick woollen coats, even though their proximity to the fire shouldn't necessitate it, are sharing a table with two spare chairs.

"You get the drinks, I'll get our seats," Katie says, and she makes her way over.

She's too quick off the mark for me to tell her not to.

I'm still staring at her when the barmaid repeats herself.

"Did you want a drink or are you just here to lean on the bar?"

"Oh sorry, yes. I'll have a…" I look along the taps, trying to work out what the options are. "What ale do you have, sorry?"

"Ale? We have bottles. Cider on tap."

"Cider," I repeat, unhelpfully. When in Rome, I suppose. "Sure. A pint of whatever is good, please."

"They're all good," she replies. Her face is deadpan. I'm making a great impression.

"Um…" I fluster, and look at the label closest to me. "Dandy Boy, sure. Sounds great. I'll take a pint of that."

"Dandy Boy," she repeats, and I catch the man to my left sharing a smirk with her.

Maybe I'm being paranoid. I try to ignore it. Her dirty-blonde curls nod forward as she focuses on pulling my pint, and I turn and look over at Katie while I have a second to spare. Sure enough, she has settled into the seat next to the man on the wall side of the table. There's a trestle bench with a velvet-covered cushion beneath her. I get a bare wooden chair opposite. At least I do if they don't mind me crashing their party too.

"Anything else?"

I hear her the first time and turn quickly to reply.

"Wine, please. Dry white wine. Better make it a large, please."

"Large," she repeats. This parroting seems to be her thing. She doesn't ask me what type I would prefer, so she has either decided that I am clueless and there is no point asking, or they only have one kind. Either way, she turns to the fridge below the counter, pulls out a bottle, and pours out Katie's drink.

"Just those?" she says as she plonks the wine glass next to the cider.

"Yes, thanks."

I pull out my wallet and get my debit card from its slot. She waves the card machine in my direction without telling me how much the round costs. I guess I should have waited to be told, but I'm too embarrassed to ask now, so I make the contactless payment and let it go.

"Thanks," I say, and try to make my smile look genuine.

She turns away and moves back up the bar to continue the chat that I interrupted.

"You're drinking?" Katie says, as I set the glasses down on the table.

"I'll be okay with one," I say. "Maybe two. It's a straight road from here to the cabin, and there's no one else likely to be around."

She's about to argue the point when the man next to me surprises me by turning to us and speaking.

"Staying in the cabin, are you?"

"What?" I say. Of course I heard him, but I'm taken off-guard by the fact that he is talking to me.

"We are," Katie says. Her voice is like honey; she's always so charming with strangers. That's probably how she hooked me in, that sweet trap, like flypaper.

The man nods and turns back to his friend.

I mouth *weird* in Katie's direction and she gives me a wide-eyed shrug in return.

"How's your wine?" I ask.

She takes a gulp. "Well, it's cold," she says. "It's okay. It'll taste better by my third glass, I'm sure."

I smile and reach across the table to hold her hand.

"This was a good idea," I say. "It's good to be out of the house." I pause, and add, "It's good to be out for drinks with you. It's been too long."

There's another pause, this time from her, before she replies. We are both being cautious with our words, thinking through our moves carefully, and trying not to say things that will sour the atmosphere. It's like being at the poker table again, thinking through how I am going to play my hand. You'll probably have heard the old adage that it's not the hand you are dealt but the way you play it that matters. In much the same way, I am trying to think of the best way to handle my thoughts, my words and my actions to have the optimal outcome with Katie. I am always playing a game, even when I am not at the table.

"We could start having regular date nights," she says. "When we get home. Maybe once a week…or…" She stops. I guess that she is wondering whether she is overplaying her hand and asking for too much too soon. If she raises the stakes too high, I might fold.

I shake my head. "Once a week would be good. I can take a night off when you aren't on shift, and we can go out somewhere."

"Or stay home together." She smiles and squeezes my fingers.

She looks beautiful. She's by far the most attractive woman in this room; she's probably the most attractive woman in this village. The light glints off the silver necklace that she has strung around her neck. She always wears it, but it's usually tucked away beneath a T-shirt or a shirt or her uniform. She takes it off at bedtime and clips it back every morning. It's a thick cross shape, with a tiny screw fastening at the bottom. To the casual observer it looks like a standard reasonably pretty crucifix. I know though that inside it she carries fragments of her mother's ashes.

She catches me looking and raises her hand from her glass to touch the cold metal. I stroke her other hand and pat it softly.

"I know," I say, and she gives me a gentle smile.

We look at each other in silence, connected by our hands and by our thoughts.

Again, we are interrupted by our table-share companions. This time, the man next to Katie speaks.

"Have you seen her?" he says.

"Sorry, what?" My voice is snappier than I intended. I was deep in my thoughts of Katie's all-too-recent loss, and trying to find the words to talk to her. I'm in no mood for conversation with strangers, but then again, I rarely am.

Katie lets go of my grip and waves her hand subtly in a *calm down* gesture.

"Have you seen her?" he says again in exactly the same tone, and with exactly the same expression on his face.

I look at him, and then at his friend, who is also staring, apparently waiting for my response. I'm aware, suddenly, of a sense of unease, a change in atmosphere in the bar. I look around and see the barmaid has stopped her conversation to focus on us. The man she was talking to has also cast his eyes on Katie and me. The two men playing dominos have taken a break to watch us.

I take a drink from my cider and clear my throat.

"I can see that you don't like outsiders here," I say. "Perhaps it would be better if my girlfriend and I…"

Katie shakes her head silently. I start to get to my feet and the man to my side puts his hand onto my shoulder, pressing me back down into my seat.

"No need for that, my friend," he says flatly.

"Have you seen her?" the other man asks again.

Katie tries to rescue the situation by replying to the question that I have been asked three times already. "Seen *who* exactly?" She keeps her tone neutral and inquisitive. She's a far better diplomat than I.

I decide to keep my pint in my hands and busy myself on drinking that and let Katie deal with this.

The two men look at each other. The one next to me turns around to look at the barmaid, and I follow his gaze to see her nod.

"The woman," he says. "The woman in the woods."

I was going to keep quiet, but when he says this, I have to reply. "Like…" I wave my arm. "This place. That's the name of the pub, right?"

"The name of the pub," he nods, and the man across from him nods too.

The second man, next to Katie, continues. "Pubs are named after things though. Things don't be named after pubs."

This is like some strange riddle that I don't want to be caught up in. Date night with Katie seems to have become somewhat surreal. I tip my glass in their direction, first one and then the other and take another drink.

Katie tries her best.

"So, who is the woman?" she asks, and apparently that is the right question.

"Who is the woman?" The man next to her asks the man opposite, or at least he repeats Katie's question.

"You haven't heard the story then?"

I think it's probably clear to everyone in the bar that are standing silently staring at us by this point that no, we haven't heard whatever story it is that this man so clearly wants to tell us.

Katie smiles, and shakes her head. "I'm afraid we haven't. We only arrived yesterday, and…"

"Only yesterday," he nods, interrupting her. "Only yesterday."

"And you haven't seen the woman?" the other man says. It's more of a statement than as question, as the first man starts talking again straight away.

"It's for the best," he says. "Best that you don't see her."

"Bad things happen," says the other man. "Bad things happen when she's disturbed."

Katie is still trying to smile, but I can see the curve of her lips faltering.

"Okay," I say, breaking in. "This is all very interesting, but we came for a quiet drink and…"

The barmaid rings the last orders bell and I look at the clock above the bar. It's nine-thirty. Unless they keep very different hours here, it's a long way from being last orders.

"Everybody out," she shouts. "Come on. Out."

I shake my head at Katie, start to down my pint, and feel slightly relieved that we are going to leave.

The two men next to us abandon their pints and get to their feet.

"Be careful," one of them says.

"Be careful," the other repeats, as he steps around the side of the table and the two of them make for the door.

"You were right," Katie says in a hushed voice. "Very weird."

I start to stand, and feel a firm warm hand grip my arm.

"Not you two," the barmaid says. "Better that you hear the whole story and hear the truth of it."

The rest of the customers are filing out of the front door obediently, in a way that I could never imagine anyone doing in town. I once sat at a poker table with the casino fire alarm going off and in the face of a possible emergency no one stood to leave. All it takes here is for this short woman in her mid-forties to ring a bell and issue a command, and everyone goes home. She must have some powers I don't know about.

"Perhaps we had better…" I start to speak.

"Sit," she says.

Katie nods at me, and so I sit. The barmaid sits into the chair beside me.

"I wouldn't trust those two not to fill your heads with a load of nonsense," the woman says. "How long are you staying in the cabin for?"

"Five nights," Katie says. "This is our second."

The woman settles back into her chair and takes a mouthful of the pint that her customer left.

"Okay," she says. "How rude of me. I haven't even introduced myself. I'm Carla. I own this place."

"You own it and work the bar?" I ask. "Seb," I say. "And this is Katie."

"Katie, hello." Carla extends a hand across the table and the women shake, then Carla takes my hand and holds it. "Blackheath shouldn't be letting people stay in that cabin," she says. "No good will come of it."

My previous thoughts resurface. They don't like out-of-towners. To some extent I can't say that I blame them. It's obviously a very small, close community, and city folk coming in spending money to invade their village on a little jaunt in the country can't be very pleasant for them.

"Who is the woman?" Katie asks again.

Carla takes a long deep drink of the pint, draining the glass, and sets it back onto the table. Then she reaches across to pick up the three-quarter full pint that belonged to the other man and puts that in front of her.

"It's a two-pint kind of story, but this will have to do," she says. Then she takes a breath, exhales and begins.

"Eighteen years ago, there was a villager called Annabel Harford."

I flick my eyes over to Katie and she shakes her head, almost imperceivably. I contain a small sigh and take another sip of my cider, wishing I had more.

"Beautiful, she was. Everyone adored her. Some adored her a little bit too much, if you know what I mean. She was too kind, she was. Too kind." The barmaid takes another mouthful of cider. "She got caught up with the wrong sort of man. An out-of-towner he was, just like you. He came and he met her, and he stayed, and everything was going well for her, or so it seemed until she got herself with child."

Nobody really talks like this, I think. It feels like I have stepped back into some strange parallel universe. Still, I go along with it.

"He didn't stick around much after that. Moved off back to the city."

I wonder if she means London, or maybe the next nearest town to here. There definitely aren't any cities within a seventy-mile radius, or there would have been a casino closer, and we probably wouldn't have ended up here.

Katie nods encouragingly and Carla continues.

"The child, a little girl, Audrey, she was as beautiful as her mother. Not a trace of that man in her. Annabel did her best, and the village, well, we all stick together out here, we helped her out, did what we could, did our best for the both of them." She stands up and keeps talking while she walks to the bar, picks up a bottle of vodka from behind it and walks back over to her seat. "Couldn't do enough though, could we?" She pours a hefty measure of vodka into the dirty glass and knocks it back.

"What happened?" Katie asks.

'*Why are you telling us this?*' I think but don't say.

Carla pours another double shot, and offers the bottle to Katie, and then to me. Katie covers her glass with her hand in refusal and I shake my head. Carla shrugs.

"I'm getting to that," she says. "One day, when the little girl was three years old, Annabel took her out into Blackheath's woods. Off to pick the wimberries they were. There are plenty right here in the village. I don't know why she felt like she had to go down there picking when there are enough here for everyone, but she said they were the best, the biggest, the juiciest, and I didn't feel strongly enough about it to be arguing with her. Headstrong she was." She shakes her head and takes more vodka. "Headstrong. I should have told her, or I should have gone with her."

"What happened?" Katie prompts again.

She's impatient. I'm bored. I'm picking at the edge of the beermat, flipping it on the edge of the table, wondering how long this is going to go on for.

"Well, they d-d-disappeared." She stutters the word as if it is painful to say, like a razor blade passing from her lips. "Both of them. Like the ground opened up and swallowed them. Disappeared." This time the word comes out in a choking sob.

Katie leans across the table and grabs Carla's hands, trying to comfort this stranger in a strange place with her strange story.

"We looked for them, we all looked for them. The whole village, the police, everyone. It was in all the newspapers around here for months, for all the time that we were searching." She looks at me as if to ask if I had heard anything about it, but I haven't and I shrug.

"I blamed myself, of course. I should have warned her. I should never have let her go out there alone."

"Did they…did you ever find them?" Katie asks. She is enthralled by this. She loves a good story. I suppose that's another of the reasons that she likes working in the care home. All those old dears with their long lives, filled with story after story. Katie laps it up, she's a great listener.

Carla shakes her head and raises her hand to her mouth covering it. Her eyes are spilling tears down her red, veiny cheeks. Her mascara is running in thick black rivulets.

"Hey," Katie says. She reaches into her tiny purse and pulls out a clean tissue. "Here." She dabs at Carla's face until Carla takes over.

"Thanks," she breathes.

"So, if Annabel...if they're dead..." I begin, but Carla cuts back in.

"She's been seen. Out there. In the woods."

Carla speaks in a way that makes her already dramatic words border on melodrama.

"So, there's a ghost. The woods are haunted by Annabel's ghost, eternally seeking her lost daughter, Audrey?" I try to conceal my scepticism, but it's difficult.

Katie is lapping it up though. "Haunted," she says, looking at me with what I can only interpret as excitement.

Carla opens her mouth, but I can't hold back.

"I'm so sorry," I say, standing up. "But I don't believe in ghosts. When you're dead, you're dead. If they were never found..." I let the sentence trail off again.

Carla nods.

"Then she really can't be wandering around the woods. I know you probably enjoy telling this story to out-of-towners, and maybe some of them are scared enough to pack up and leave, but…"

"Shut up, Seb," Katie says, kicking my shin hard beneath the table. "Sit down and shut up."

"No, you can go. Just get out. Go," Carla spits.

She's lost it with me, I can see that. There's no going back to the ghost story now.

"I'm so sorry," Katie says. She leans towards the barmaid, who has slouched into a huddle over her bottle of vodka.

"Katie. There is no such thing as a ghost. This is ridiculous. You saw what it was like when we walked in here, everyone stopped and stared at us as if we stank of shit. We aren't wanted here, and this woman seemingly has the job of getting rid of us. This Annabel woman probably never even existed. It's just a way to use the name of the pub to scare townies out of the place."

Katie is pushing me towards the door, trying to stop me from upsetting Carla further.

As we tumble onto the street, I hear Carla's parting words to us, broken by heaving sobs.

"She did exist. She was my sister."

That final word is flung at us like a missile.

"You're such a dick," Katie says to me and pushes me up the street towards the car.

"How was I supposed to know?" I mumble, like it's some kind of excuse.

I know it though. I am a dick. I am an asshole. I know.

Chapter Six

Back in the cabin, the atmosphere is as cold as the night outside. Katie has taken the sofa, her legs extended across it in a clear statement that I am not welcome to sit with her. I am on the armchair, which is surprisingly wide and very comfortable, so I'm not actually complaining. Dex paces from one of us to the other at regular intervals before settling by our sides, trying not to show any allegiance to either party. He is neutral, impartial, because he knows that's the best way for him to be. He has been through this before, of course. He has sat through the post-war period of many Pie and Bun Bun fights. He knows how this goes.

Katie is reading a book, so she is completely unfazed by the chill between us. I have my phone, and I am pretty tempted to log into an online poker site and play a few hands, but I promised Katie that I wouldn't. Not while we were here. Despite the fact that she isn't talking to me, I still wouldn't feel right. Instead, I have clicked open my web browser and I am doing a little amateur detective work.

Of course, I don't believe in ghosts, that would be ridiculous, but if someone did go missing in the woods here, well that appeals to my morbid curiosity. I type into the search box: **blackheath culloton disappearance**

There are a few news reports. "Police search woods after woman and child disappear." "Underwater search in connection with 2002 disappearance". Underwater? I didn't even know we were near a lake or river. "Police appeal to find missing Culloton woman after 'out of character' disappearance". Is there such a thing as an 'in-character' disappearance? I try to imagine. "Oh yes, the woman and child vanished, but it was just like them to do something like that." It doesn't make any sense. "Local landowner interviewed in missing mother and daughter case." I click on that header and read through the article.

Local landowner Roman Blackheath has been questioned by police in connection with missing Culloton woman Annabel Harford and her three-year-old daughter Audrey. Harford's sister, Carla Frampton, of the Rose and Garter public house, reported that Annabel had been planning to gather fruit on Blackheath's estate at the time of her disappearance.

Harford did not return home and has not been in contact with friends or relatives since.

There's a photograph of a dark-haired woman, pale-skinned with piercing blue eyes crouched beside a toddler. Clearly her daughter. She looks very much like the woman on the sigh that now hangs outside the renamed *Rose and Garter*. It strikes me as a little odd that Carla would rebrand her pub in a constant reminder of what happened to her sister, but maybe it's the only way she has of keeping her memory alive in the history of the village.

I go back to the web search results and keep scrolling.

"Police call off search for missing woman after body is found."

So, there it is. They found Annabel's body. What about the child? I swipe my finger down the screen, trying to find more information.

"Body found in hunt for missing woman" – Annabel, not the child.

"Family heartbroken after body found in Culloton case" – again, Annabel.

I hear a laboured sigh from the sofa. Katie shuffles noisily, changing position, obviously trying to get my attention without actually talking to me. She puts her book down, moves her legs, curling them under her, picks up her mug from the little table next to her, puts it down again. I look at her, over the top of my phone. Dexter trots over, obediently, to take his position on the floor beside her, and she trails her hand down to pet him, a pained expression on her face.

"Do you need anything?" I say.

I have to be the one to break this impasse. I know that she isn't going to speak first.

She makes a humming, sighing noise but doesn't reply. She doesn't even look at me.

I roll my eyes and click my phone closed. I could have carried on with my research quite happily, but I am here to try to repair this relationship, so I need to direct my attention to Katie.

"I'm sorry about earlier." I sit on the edge of the chair, my body angled towards her, open and non-defensive. I know a lot about body language, and I want to give her all the signs that I genuinely mean what I say. "I really was an idiot. I was rude to that lady, Carla, and I know I spoiled our evening. So, I'm sorry, Katie Pie. Tell me what I need to do to make this better and I'll do it. Anything."

She looks down at her book as if I haven't spoken. Dex sticks his warm pink tongue out from between his teeth and licks gently at her hand.

"Katie?" I say, in my most conciliatory tone. "I am sorry. Please."

She lets Dex lick her and strokes his head softly in return. That's a positive sign. She is thawing, I know it.

I pause, take a breath, and stand up.

"Let me fix you a drink, or…"

She glares at me, but I walk towards her anyway. I'm moving now, I can't stop in my tracks and sit back down, that would be admitting defeat. I'm committed to my action.

"Can I get you something?" I crouch by her side, on the floor next to Dexter, and place my hand onto her arm. "I'm sorry. I mean it. I'm sorry."

"You were awful," she says.

"Yes," I reply. "Yes, I was."

I've learned, from years of experience, that sometimes the best thing to do is to agree. Even if I don't always believe what it is that I am agreeing with, in the short term, and sometimes also in the long term, it is better to agree. Okay, so it might seem like I am giving in and losing, but I am winning peace. I am winning something more important than one little argument.

She looks at me and shakes her head.

"That poor woman," she says. She sets her book down on the table and brings her legs down in front of her to settle on the floor, almost squashing Dex, who darts quickly out of the way. "She lost her sister and her niece, and all you could do was...I don't even know what you think you were doing."

"I..." I try to think of a reasonable explanation. "I don't believe in ghost stories, and it felt like, I mean I thought..." I'm garbling, trying to make excuses. "I thought she just wanted us out of there. You saw what the old guys were like when we walked in. They probably do that to all of the visitors. People in small villages, they are..." Weird? Odd? Eccentric? Dangerous? "Different. They aren't like us, Katie, and we aren't like them." I'm getting close to starting another argument here, I can tell, so I slow down. "I'm sorry. I should have listened. I should have been more polite."

"Yes, you should. Her poor sister and that little girl. Lost in the woods. I can't even imagine. How awful." She shuffles again slightly, more alert now. Then she asks me what I know she has been wanting to ask me since we hurried out of the pub. "What do you think happened?"

There wasn't much of an explanation, from what I have managed to read so far. The two of them went missing, there was a search, and eventually the mother's body was found. No real suspects, although Roman Blackheath was questioned and never charged with anything. I tell Katie what I know, which isn't much at all.

"What do you think, though? I haven't been able to concentrate on reading, I just keep thinking about it. The girl got pregnant and the father dumped her. Do you think he was involved in some way? That he came back to get rid of her, and take the child? They never found a child's body?"

"I haven't read anywhere that they did yet, no."

"And they never arrested anyone? No one was ever charged with the murder?"

"I couldn't see that they ever said it was murder. Remember it was a long time ago. I found those few articles, but the information is patchy at best. We could probably find out more if we knew where to look."

"Or we could have asked Carla if you hadn't pissed her off so much."

"I'm surprised she wanted to tell her as much as she did already, to be honest. What was all that about? It was the guys next to us that started it, wasn't it? *'Have you seen her?'*" I mimic the man's broad country accent.

"Carla said it too though. *'She's been seen'*. Surely she doesn't believe that. She must know that her sister is dead. Wishful thinking, you reckon?"

I shrug. "Maybe."

"And maybe it is her ghost. Always searching for the body of her child." She says it in her best scary-story voice, and I laugh. "What?" she says. "It could be."

I try to keep a straight face as I realise that she means it.

"Okay, Katie. Okay. If that's what you want to believe."

"You think that when we are dead, we are dead, and that's it?" She's reached up to the chain around her neck, and she's rubbing the cross between her fingers.

"Oh Pie. I know you want to believe that your mum is still here, that her spirit is still with us." I speak as calmly as I can, controlling my tone, trying to conceal my feelings. "I don't believe the same things as you though. I do think that when we die, that's it. Hey, it doesn't mean that you have to think what I do."

It's too late, I've said too much, and tears are flooding down her face.

Two years it has been since her mother died. Two years. She's not even begun to get over it. I know that things were tough for her, growing up, and that her mother helped her through a lot, but I don't know all of the detail and I'm not sure I ever will. I know that her mother was the only family she had, and that when she died a part of Katie was destroyed along with her. I know, but I don't know how to talk to Katie about it, I don't know if she wants to talk about it yet, or if I would be the best person to talk to. I love her, I do love her so much, but I know my limitations.

"I know how much you loved her," I say.

I can't stop myself from talking, can I? I've already said too much.

"I love her. I love her now. I didn't stop loving her just because she died. You don't understand anything. You don't even try to understand. I'm going to bed. You stay out here. I don't want to be near you again tonight. Just…just think about what you want and think about…just think about who you are."

With that she slams her feet on the floor and flounces off down the corridor to the bedroom.

Dexter looks at me with his big chocolate melt eyes as if to say, *"you're really fucking this up, Seb,"* and I know that he is right.

Chapter Seven

After an uncomfortable night sleeping on the sofa, I'm even more determined to put things right with Katie. I can't bear to do that again, and well, I'm meant to be making things better between us rather than worse. I put on my boots and head out to the very edge of the woods, while Dex takes a pee against the nearest tree.

"I promise we'll get a long walk later," I tell him.

He stops for a second and then wanders off in a circuit around the cabin. I've come out for flowers. There is some part of me, buried quite deeply, but present nonetheless, that knows how to be romantic. Well, I've seen movies and I have read about this kind of thing, so I assume it's what women like. I don't really have an eye for flower arranging though, and I have no idea which of the available plants I should pick. There are clusters of small daffodil-looking plants, and a few patches of tiny white specks that I think are snowdrops. They aren't very impressive. I want roses or tulips or something showy like that, but I guess they aren't the sort of things that grow here. I remember that not far into the woods the sides of the makeshift path were lined with a patchy blue carpet that I know must be bluebells. I call Dex, and we trudge in so that I can collect a decent bunch. They smell fresh and light, and they look pretty. Just what I wanted.

Dex wants to run on ahead, of course, now that we have broached the treeline, but I shake my head and tell him, "Later". He hangs his tail between his legs and looks at me as if I am a terrible person. I'm used to that look, but more used to seeing it from Katie.

"Later, I promise." I pet him before striding off back towards the cabin, a large bunch of the blue flowers in my grasp.

I can't see a vase in any of the kitchen cupboards, but I pull out a plain water jug and make do. It looks country-like, and I'm pleased by the effect. It's almost as though I planned it.

I boil the kettle, toast the bread, and set butter and jam onto a large pine tray. Someone with better presentation skills or more experience at this kind of thing would probably decant some jam into a little bowl or root around for a butter dish, but even setting this up in the first place is really the extent of my talents. The toast pops, the kettle clicks, and I complete the composition. The jug of bluebells is really too heavy and big to take along on the tray, but I do it anyway, thinking I can set it onto the table before Katie wakes.

"Wish me luck," I say to Dex.

He wags his tail supportively.

It doesn't come naturally to me, being romantic, making big gestures like this, or even putting someone else's feelings ahead of my own. Before I was with Katie, I was a loner. I wasn't really interested in socialising. When the guys from Vesper went out, I would make excuses, which were usually completely factual, and mostly focused upon the fact that the nights that they wanted to go on a pub crawl were mainly the nights that I wanted to be at the casino, taking advantage of guys like them who had ended up drunk and willing to throw away money on a few badly played hands of poker. Not that they ever showed up there, but I would have loved to take money off several of those assholes. So, yeah, I'm not a people person. I'm not a person person. Luckily, Katie knows that, so when I kneel, stroke the hair from her face, waking her up, and gesture towards the tray I've set on the bedside table, she is way more impressed than, say, if a regular boyfriend had done this. Her eyes widen, and I hope that she has forgotten what happened last night, or at least she can set it to the side, and we can try to push past it.

"I suppose you think that this makes everything okay?" She opens both eyes, and glares at me, but behind the stern expression, I can see the trace of a smile.

"No. No. Of course not," I say. I've learnt this move; I know what to do in spots like this. "I wanted to do something to make you happy. I love you so much, Pie."

I lean to kiss her, knowing that this is the key moment. If she accepts, then she can't stay mad at me. If she pushes me away, we are set for a morning of misery, maybe even a full day of it. My lips make contact with hers. She is so warm, and despite just having woken up she tastes sweet and delicious. I can't stop myself from feeling a rush of…love? Lust? Something. Something stirs inside me, but now is not the time. Get things back on track first. Get the car back on the road before you start trying to show off spinning donuts.

"Okay," she says. "Seeing as we are meant to be here to be together and do our very best to work at this, just because of that, I forgive you."

I didn't even have to grovel and apologise. This really must be important to her. I'm actually quite touched. Not that I have ever doubted that she wants to be with me. I mean she has put up with me and stuck with me this long, so she must either be crazy, or crazy about the idiot that is Seb Archer. Five whole years. She should get a medal.

"Thanks, Pie." I kiss her again, and then reach for her hand, pull her up, and share breakfast.

"I haven't taken Dex out yet," I say, between bites of the toast. "I was thinking we could go out together today?"

She shrugs, still chewing, and nods. A few crumbs have fallen onto the place between her collarbone and the top of her breast, and I want to reach out, touch them, wipe them off, and then keep moving my hand down.

She catches me staring, and smiles.

"Sure. I'd like that." She pulls the cover up higher. I'm forgiven, but I don't seem to have had my privileges reinstated yet. "We could take out a picnic if you like."

I try to stop myself from frowning, but my reluctance must show. My idea of being out in the woods is jumping over logs, climbing mossy rocks, pretending I'm some kind of action hero. Hers is something out of a fairy story, where we find a circle of sunlight between the trees, and sit with the foxes and rabbits, all one big happy family, eating our triangle-cut sandwiches. I know that foxes and rabbits don't behave in real life the same way they behave in the Disney films that she still likes to watch, despite having turned thirty last year.

Also, I know that if we take a picnic, I will be the one that has to carry it.

"Maybe," I say, and mask my expression by wiping my face with the back of my hand, turning away to pick up my mug.

"Or I could make us something good when we get back, seeing as you put this lovely breakfast together."

Either she picked up on my reticence or she is very easily impressed. When you're used to such a low baseline of effort from your boyfriend, I'm sure that little things could seem very impressive.

I kiss her again and get to my feet.

"Listen, take your time, get yourself up and dressed, and we can head out whenever you are ready," I say.

Dex is standing in the doorway, watching expectantly. I want to give Katie some space, but more importantly I don't want to give her the chance to start going over what happened last night.

As I get to the door, Katie calls my name.

"Do you…" She starts to say something and then seems to change her mind.

"What? Do I what?"

She shakes her head. "It doesn't matter."

I turn again and I'm two steps into the hallway when she shouts.

"Do you think there could be a ghost in the woods?"

I'm glad she waited until I left, because I don't think I would have been able to keep a straight face if she had asked me in the bedroom. I stop myself from showing the laughter in my voice.

"No, Pie. I don't think there could be a ghost in the woods." I repeat her words so that I can repeat her tone, echo it back to her rather than letting my brain start to fire off cynicism and sarcasm.

I stand still, waiting for more, but she is silent, and I am glad.

I know that it's been hard for her since her mum died, and perhaps I have humoured her a little too much when she has talked about her *being in a better place* or mentioned that she has felt her mother's presence. I may be an asshole, but I can keep it under control sometimes.

Katie takes her usual hour to get dressed and emerges from the bedroom looking like she's ready to go for a lunch date in town with one of her girls rather than a trek through the woods. I pause before speaking, and instead of what I wanted to say I make do with, "You look beautiful." Not practical in any way, but beautiful. She has showered and done whatever it is that she does with her hair to make it curly and bouncy. It's naturally pretty flat, or straight or whatever, but when she's going somewhere special, she spends time on it, making it, well, more like this. She either sees her and I taking a walk in the woods as a special occasion or she has already got to the point where she would rather spend time on her own in the bedroom making unnecessary aesthetic adjustments than being out here talking to me. I hope it's the former.

"Thanks," she smiles, and walks over.

She flings her arms around me and presses her head against my chest. When she's just finished putting on her make-up, she always does this thing where she makes sure she presses her hair against me rather than burying her face into me. Whether it's against my shoulder or my chest, she always puts the thought into avoiding smudging her make-up, rather than enjoying the embrace without worrying about her foundation. I stroke her hair and kiss the top of her head.

She's wearing jeans today, at least, that's one small concession. On her top half she has a white vest and a flimsy floaty floral shirt over the top. If it's as cold as it has been so far this week, she's going to freeze. I have to make the choice between asking her if she's taking a jacket and risk an argument, or to say nothing and know that I will probably end up lending her my coat within the next half hour. I'm wearing jeans, T-shirt and hoody, in my usual style less style, and I calculate that if I have to pass over my jacket, I'll probably just about be warm enough. Anything to avoid conflict.

She's about to slip her feet into the Birkenstocks by the door, when she sees me putting on my walking boots.

"Not wearing your nice trainers?" she asks. It sounds like she thinks I'm not making an effort, somehow. Like she has dressed up for our 'date' and I am slacking by being practical.

"It's muddy down the tracks," I say, without any suggestion that she should make a better decision about her footwear.

She pauses, kicks her sandals back against the wall, and hops back down to the bedroom.

"Don't want to fuck those up. I'll find something else. Sorry Bun Bun. Won't be a minute."

"Fine," I call after her.

"I'll grab my jacket too."

It's always, ALWAYS, better to let Katie come to her own good decisions rather than helping her to make them. She's not a girl who takes guidance well. I'm not sure if her upbringing was too strict, or she just likes to rebel in general, but there's definitely something ingrained in her. I don't want to unpackage what it is, I just want to respect it and not stir things up.

She comes happily bobbing back towards me wearing trainers that are more dressy than sensible, but still, they're far better than the open-toed sandals that she had planned to wear. She's got her parka on now, hood up, staring out at me beneath the fur trim. Something about it makes her look vulnerable and absolutely sexy as hell. More importantly at this moment, she looks warm and I'm not going to have to give up my own jacket for her. Win-win.

Dex has been pacing up and down waiting for us to open the door, and when I finally do, he bolts off.

"Dex!" I call after him. After yesterday, I want to keep a closer eye on him, watch where he's going, more to the point, watch where we are going. If I stepped into a rabbit snare, or God forbid Katie did, then...well, it doesn't bear thinking about.

He pretends not to hear me and lollops onwards. I shoot a worried look at Katie.

"Perhaps I should have put him on his lead today."

"Dexter!" she shouts, and this time he stops in his tracks. He looks back over his shoulder, and patiently waits for us to catch up with him. She gives me a smug little smile, and I let her have the satisfaction. Far better that he is safe, and she is smug.

When we reach his side, I squat to clip the lead onto his collar, and ruffle his fur.

"Don't want you getting hurt again," I say softly into his ear. He seems to be walking, and running, without any evidence of yesterday's injury.

Katie holds out her hand to take the lead, and I hand it over.

I let Katie walk on, Dex by her side, and I keep as close behind her as I can on the narrow, mulchy path. She's talking to me, or perhaps to Dex, and every now and again I make a general, non-committal response. I can't actually hear what she's saying, but it doesn't really matter. We are spending time together, she is not unhappy, and keeping it that way feels like the optimal play.

We pass the patch of bluebells, and as she sees them, she turns, points, and gives me a wide, stunning smile. Sometimes I get it right.

I'm keeping my eyes to the track, trying to watch out for any signs of danger, but I think that as long as we keep to the path all three of us will be just fine. It's not fun for Dexter to have to stay on his leash, but at least I know how he feels. I'm on my best behaviour, toeing the line, falling into formation.

"What was that?" Katie stops, and Dex stands obediently at her side.

I didn't notice anything, but Dexter obviously did. His fur bristles, and he's sniffing at the air anxiously.

"What? Did you see something? Hear something?" I look around, but there's nothing jumping out at me as unusual.

"No, I mean, yes. I don't know what –"

Then I hear it, and Dexter does too. He starts to make that low hum from deep within his gut. His teeth show, he's poised, ready to spring. Someone, something, moving through the trees.

Katie lowers her voice to a whisper. "Can you see anything? An animal? A person?"

Where we are standing, here on the path, is well concealed; we wouldn't exactly be easy to see if there was something or someone here that wanted to see us. The trees are close to the track, not very well spaced. This woodland feels natural, rather than a planned, planted estate. That also means that it's not particularly easy to see anything in the woods either.

It's off to our left, the sound. All I know is that it's movement. There's something there.

"Ssh. Just wait. Can't be anything dangerous, out here." I speak as quietly and calmly as I can.

Logically, there really aren't many dangerous animals out here, so we should let whatever it is pass, and move cautiously along.

Katie's face changes. "Perhaps it's a deer. Seb, Seb." She tugs on my sleeve, more excited now than concerned.

"I hope it's a deer. I'd love to see one. A stag, maybe. Big antlers…" She's up on her tiptoes now, straining to see.

"Maybe, Pie. Maybe." For some reason, I have a sense of unease. I don't feel safe. I reason with myself. I'm not used to being out in the woods, I'm not used to being amidst nature. After that shit with the snare yesterday, I'm on edge.

Then she tugs again. The colour has drained from her face, or she has the kind of look that tells me that below the make-up she's ashen.

"What if it's HER?" she says. "What if it's the ghost?"

Whatever I think might be running through the undergrowth, it's certainly not a ghost.

I take a breath, and pull her in towards me, hugging her, comforting her, and again concealing my expression.

"Honey Pie, there aren't any ghosts. There really aren't any ghosts. Okay?" I pull back so that I can see her face. "Okay?" I say again. I want to hear her say it. I need to hear it. I can't let this carry on.

"But…" She stops herself and shakes her head. "What if there are?"

"Oh, Pie." I kiss her again. "It's an animal. Some kind of cute little animal. Nothing scary, nothing dangerous, nothing bad. And it is definitely not a ghost."

I believe that it's not a ghost, I absolutely completely believe that, but the rest of it, well, I'm not exactly one hundred percent certain about. I tick off a mental checklist in my head of all the things it could be, while I look over the top of Katie's head into the dense tree-lined horizon. Dexter is tugging on his lead, and Katie pulls him back in towards her.

"It's okay, Dex," she says, reaching down to stroke him and reassure him. "It's nothing. There's no such thing as ghosts."

I know that she's only trying to comfort herself, as she squats next to him and strokes him with both hands.

"Pie. Pie, really. It's okay."

Dexter is probably winding her up more than anything, as he is still on full alert. He gives her face one long lick, and then tugs, breaks free of her grip, and darts off into the trees.

"Oh no! Dex, no! Come back!" I yell, even though my instincts had been to stay silent and still. "Dexter!"

Katie has started to cry. "I'm sorry. He just...he pulled away, he...I wasn't holding on to him properly. I'm sorry, Seb."

I can't handle her sobbing right now, so I grab her hand, pull her to her feet and kiss her again. It seems like my go-to action at the moment. I don't have anything particularly useful to say, so I use my mouth in the best way I can think of.

"Ssh. I'll go and get him."

I look around, trying to find a safe place to leave Katie while I go and recover Dex, and maybe find whatever is the source of the disturbance. It will probably turn out to be a rabbit and we will all feel like idiots. Apart from Dexter, perhaps, who will probably love the chase that could ensue.

"Here. Sit here." I take a few steps down the path and gesture to a log that's lying not far off the track. It's dirty, wet and the bark is green, but it looks like as good a place as any.

"No!" Katie is adamant. "I'm going with you. You're not leaving me here on my own when there's…"

She still hasn't let go of the ghost thing then. Great.

Exasperated, I sigh, turn my head to look for Dex, who is out of sight now, but I can hear where he's got to.

"I have to get after him, and we have to hurry. I don't..."

"You don't want me slowing you down?"

"I don't want anything to happen to you Pie. I don't want you to slip or trip or anything, you know. I don't want you to get hurt. I'm trying to look after you but…" I look back to the left again. "I have to go after Dex, and I have to go now."

I start off away from the track, waving my hand in front of me, to push the low branches of the trees out of my way. They are some kind of pine trees, and there are little cones clinging to the lower, browning boughs like tiny limpets. I turn round and Katie is standing, staring, watching me hurry away. I press on, a few more paces, and then turn again.

"Okay. Come on then," I say. I'll probably regret it but taking her along beats the mood that she will be in later if I leave her behind. I can just hear her now, chastising me for leaving her alone, telling me how anything could have happened to her. Blah blah blah whatever.

She doesn't break a smile, she just pushes away the same branches that I moved out of my path and runs to catch up.

"Be careful, Pie. Stick with me."

She nods. "Can you see where he's gone?"

I shake my head. "This way. Somewhere over here, but really, no idea."

"Dexter!" she shouts.

I let her do the calling as we move ahead.

The ground is a mat of fallen pine needles, a dull beige carpet beneath our feet. The further we head into the wood, the less light breaks through the canopy. Even though these are meant to be evergreen trees, there are a lot of dead needles and detritus here.

"Dexter! Dexter, come on!" Katie is keeping her voice remarkably calm, considering.

There's nothing no sign of him as we head further, deeper, and then I see it. The powder line.

I look at Katie; she hasn't noticed anything. If I hadn't seen it before I probably wouldn't have seen it this time either. What I see is just a part of it. A small patch showing through between the ground covering, but I know what it is. I want to look more closely, I want to get some more clues as to what this is, but with Dexter missing and Katie's stupid belief in ghosts or monsters or whatever it is she thinks is out here, I really have to carry on and let it go this time. If I stop to look, or if I tell Katie about what I have seen, that's going to open a whole barrel of monkeys that I have no time to deal with right now. Instead I make a mental note of our general position and keep moving. I'll come back without Katie. I'll find out for certain what the hell it is and where it goes, because to be honest its bugging the shit out of me now.

We're about two hundred feet further when I finally see him.

Dex is standing, barking menacingly at nothing, running around in a circle like he's chasing his tail or something.

"Dex. Oh Dex. Hey. Are you okay, boy? Are you okay?"

Before I can put my hand onto Katie's arm and pull her back, warn her from running out there, she goes galloping towards our dog. We haven't found whatever he was chasing, and from the way he was behaving, he hasn't either, but perhaps he thinks it's somewhere around here.

"Katie!" I half-shout, half-whisper. "Be careful!"

She turns to give me an *'okay, dumbass'* eye-roll and kneels next to Dex.

"Seb, he's shaking. Oh shit, Dex. Are you okay? Dex. It's alright now, it's alright."

She's doing her best to calm him, and I'm doing *my* best to scan the area, looking for any sign of danger. In the dim light it would be difficult to see anything particularly well. There could be something or someone concealed behind any of these trees or bushes, and I would have a tough job making them out. Whatever or whoever is out here knows this area better than we do, and they would know how to hide.

"Get it together, Seb," I tell myself.

There's not even any reason to think that whatever has wound Dex up is dangerous. Katie has got herself worked up with the talk about the stupid non-existent ghost, and Dex is just not used to being around so much nature. The only thing weird out here is that line, and there's probably a really simple explanation for it.

I'm letting myself get carried away. It's like, what do they call it when you get carried along in group mentality, I don't know, everyone else acts a certain way so you get swept up in mass hysteria. There's only the three of us and one of our group isn't even human. Still, I've been out of town for three days and I am losing it already. Well done, Seb. Now calm the hell down.

I put my hand gently onto Katie's shoulder and she jumps.

"Sorry," I say. "Didn't mean to…I didn't realise you were so…Everything is fine. I can't see anything."

I've made the decision to focus and call whatever Dexter was after a 'thing'. It's more than likely an animal, and if it did happen to be a person there's no reason to think they are malignant. They've gone now anyway. It's just the three of us again. Everything is fine.

Katie doesn't look convinced, and Dexter is still trembling. She's stroking him, whispering in his ear, but whatever is out here, he doesn't like it.

"Shall we make our way back? He's had a good run," I try to force a smile.

Katie slaps my leg sharply.

"I don't think I'll be coming out with you again," she says. "This isn't my idea of a romantic adventure."

"No," I say, truthfully. "Mine neither."

To be honest it's a relief. I would much rather have a half hour, or maybe an hour each day when it's just Dexter and me. Much as I love Katie, I do need to have some time away from her, on my own.

Chapter Eight

Even though the events of the morning are at the forefront of my mind, I know better than to discuss them with Katie. I want to take her mind off them, talk about other things, distract her from anything that might upset her, or cause her to get upset with me. It's a big ask.

Curled up on the large sofa together, Katie is lying across me, her head against my chest and her legs dangling over the arm at the other end. She doesn't look at all comfortable, but I'm upright, even though I'm trapped here beneath her.

"You okay?" I ask. What I mean is *are you okay screwed up in that ridiculous position*, but she interprets the question to mean something else.

"I don't know," she says. "A bit spooked still, I guess."

Great. Now we are going down that road. If I could move, I would kick myself.

"What do you think that was all about, earlier? With Dexter?"

She twists her neck in an even more uncomfortable-looking contortion to look up at me.

"Probably just caught the scent of something he wasn't used to," I say. Convincing myself earlier that this is the truth means that I can respond quickly and calmly now.

"Hmm," Katie says. She trails her hand gently over my chest, and I can tell she's deep in thought.

I try to think of something reassuring to say. "He's never been around other animals before. It's strange for him."

"Are you sure you didn't see anything?"

"Like what?"

She wriggles her body around, digging her elbow into my gut in the process, so that she can look me in the eyes.

"A woman?"

"Why would you ask that? Don't you think I would have told you if I had seen a bloody woman? Do you not think that I would think that it was probably worth mentioning?"

Keep calm, Seb. Keep calm. I slow myself down.

I feel her shrug, her shoulder moving against my abdomen.

"You wouldn't want to admit that you were wrong." She says it quite bluntly, there's no joking tone in her words, still, I laugh it off.

"If I had seen a woman wandering around in the woods, I would most definitely have told you." I smile, and stroke her cheek, softly. She likes that. Usually.

"Hmm." She doesn't sound convinced. She frowns and then looks over at Dex, crashed out on the rug beside us.

"Hey." I put my fingers beneath her chin and tilt her gaze back up to meet mine. "Stop thinking about it. I wish we had never gone to that stupid pub. Katie. Really. There are no such thing as ghosts. Whatever Dexter heard or smelt or whatever, it was not a ghost woman." It's starting to annoy me now. I need her to drop this.

"Those villagers though. They said…"

"I know what they said, and I am sure it must be really hard for that barmaid…

"Carla…"

"Carla…to lose her sister and niece like that, but they are dead, and she needs to let them go. Instead she has made her pub some weird memorial to them, and got the whole village worked up about it…"

Calm, Seb. Don't do this.

"Why?" Her voice is deadly serious now. "Why?"

Suddenly, she gets up, moves over to the other seat and there's a complete change in her demeanour.

"What?" I answer with another question.

"Why? Why would she do that?"

I don't know what she is getting at. I shake my head.

"I have no idea. Listen, I read up on what happened. It's all there on the internet. The woman and child went missing, just like she said. There was a big police search, and they found the bodies. Case closed. Nothing to see here. Why Carla then decided to name the pub after her, and not even in a particularly graceful way, and why everyone in the village wants to make such a crazy ghost story up is beyond me."

"To keep people out? To stop out-of-towners staying in the village?"

"Maybe." I haven't put enough thought into this. I was more interested in the facts of what had happened than trying to work what was going on in Crazytown. "But Roman is still making money off this place."

"I wonder why he needs to. I mean, he's obviously loaded, right?"

I shrug and let her continue.

"I doubt someone who owns this much land needs to make a few extra pounds from dirty weekends."

I raise my eyebrows.

"Romantic getaways then. So, if everyone wants to keep tourists away, why doesn't he?"

"I don't know. Poor people and rich people have different ideas, I guess. He might not feel the same as the general population of the village."

"Hmm," she says for the third time. "He didn't mention anything about ghosts and weird countryfolk in the advert for this place." She manages a dark laugh.

"He could put the price up a few pounds if he advertised it as a real-life spooky cabin in the woods type thing. All the cool kids love that, right? Ghosthunters and…"

I'm trying to go along with her joke, but she doesn't look impressed with the way I'm taking the conversation. I stop.

"I'm sorry, Pie."

"Okay. Okay."

A silence hangs between us for ten, twenty seconds.

"Really, I'm sorry."

"I just want to believe that there's somewhere else. I want to believe that…that she's not really gone."

She's stroking her pendant again, running her fingers over the cold silver that holds the traces of what was once her mother. So that's what this is all about. Ghosts. What lies beyond death. I should have guessed.

I never know what to say. I can never find the right words, because I don't believe. I don't believe that there is *anything* after death other than darkness, and nothingness, and the people who are left behind, trying to cope with the loss, the empty space. When Katie lost her mother, she changed. Perhaps that was the start of things going wrong between us. Indirectly it was, of course. Her change of career, my change of career. There was that, but she never dealt with her grief. She still holds on to her mother in the same way that she holds on to those ashes. Always with her. Always with us. I've never lost anyone like that, what do I know?

"She's not gone." I get off the sofa and shuffle on all fours to sit at her feet. I put my hands onto her lap and look up. "Katie. She was such a good woman. She really was. Think of all the people she helped. The impact that she had on everyone's lives. That…well, no one will forget that. No one will forget her. As long as her memory lives on, so does she. She's not physically alive, she's not a ghost or a spirit watching over you, but what she left behind, that's what matters."

Before I've even stopped talking, she is crying, crying like I have never seen before. I think for a moment that I have ruined everything, that we have come here to make our relationship better and instead I have upset her, again, just like I always do. I am such a dick. I ruin everything. Everything I touch turns to shit. I don't deserve her, this beautiful, caring, loving, fragile woman. I don't deserve to be happy with her.

"Oh Seb. Seb. Seb."

She's not pushing me away, she's not screaming at me to leave her alone, she's reaching down to me, putting her arms around me, holding me. She drops down onto the floor next to me, and we are in each other's arms, grabbing onto each other so tightly, and she is sobbing, sobbing, sobbing.

"I miss her so much. I can't stand it, Seb, I can't."

I realise, as she empties all of the tears against my chest, as she lets out the hollers and deep, bottomless sobs, that she never did this when her mother died. She has never done this in the time that has passed since. Katie is always so together, so in control. She never took the time to grieve. She has never let go, and now…now she is.

"Let it out. It's okay. It's okay."

I stroke her hair and she lets it out. She lets it all out.

Chapter Nine

The next morning, I wake up next to Katie; no more sleeping on the sofa for me. She's already scrolling through her phone when I squeeze my eyes open. Back to her old ways. Good. If it's making her happy, I'm happy.

"Anything exciting happening in the outside world?" I ask and lean up to offer a kiss. She kisses me back.

"Didn't think you were waking up today. It's nearly ten already."

"Shit! Where's Dex? Have you fed him?"

"Haven't been up yet, and he hasn't come trotting in, so…"

I snap awake. Dexter is always up by this time. At home, when Katie starts her shift at eight in the morning, he is awake at seven. Just before Katie's alarm goes off, without fail, he charges into the bedroom. When she doesn't start at eight, he still comes lolloping into the room at exactly the same time. Apparently, dogs can't work out a shift rota.

He never sleeps this late.

"Dexter?" I call. My voice sounds more panicked than I had planned.

"Hey, he's probably just tired from all the walking we've been doing. And the running he was doing when we went out yesterday."

I'm not ready to go into a discussion about all that with Katie again, so I nod, and call him again, more calmly.

A pattering of paw steps comes from the living room, his claws sounding different on the wooden floor of the lounge and then the slate of the kitchen, back to wood in the corridor. He's racing to get here, even if he has just woken up.

"Alright?" He jumps onto the bed and noses into each of us in turn, enjoying the attention. "Good sleep?" I ask him, and he wags his tail ferociously. I guess we both needed a lie in.

Katie puts her phone down and pets him.

"And to think I was going to wake you up and get you to make love to me…" Katie says.

She's teasing, I'm almost sure of it. She's not really a morning person. Not when it comes to intimacy, anyway. Trying to get any kind of action out of her before lunchtime is useless. She drags herself up for work, sure, but beyond that it's a big fat nope.

"Damn," I say, making an exaggerated face-palm gesture, and then moving from tickling Dex's belly to tickling hers.

She giggles and I kiss her. I kiss her, and kiss her, and kiss her. She seems different, somehow, today. Perhaps last night was what she needed. Being here, getting away from it all, it's given us time alone to talk about the things that we really needed to talk about. I thought it was me that was the problem. I thought it was all about Katie and me, but there was so much more than that. I couldn't see it when we were at home.

Dexter is trapped between us. He wriggles backwards, and then gives us a quick, short bark. It's one of the ways he tries to get our attention when, well, when he just wants some attention.

I smile at Katie and kiss her one last time.

"I'd better to and sort him out. Give him breakfast and take him for a run."

She nods and releases me from her grip.

"Do you want to come with us?"

I know what the answer will be before I ask. Katie may be able to get up early for work when she absolutely has to, but there's no way she's getting out of bed for physical exercise. Especially not while she is on holiday. On top of that, I really don't think yesterday's excitement was quite her thing, and I don't particularly want a repeat performance.

Then there's the line. I want to follow it. I want to find out where it leads. I can't do that with Katie.

"Thanks for asking me," she smiles, picking her phone back up.

She's in a good mood at least. I hope that it lasts. I'll do whatever it takes to keep her happy.

"I might take that bath I've been looking forward to while you're out. Don't rush back."

That suits me just fine. We only have a shower back home, so any excuse she gets to have a long soak, wherever we happen to go, she takes it. I couldn't give a toss, personally. I shower to get clean, and I don't see the point of lying in a tub full of my own dirt, but there you go. It makes her happy, so it makes me happy.

"Okay, Pie. Want me to start running it for you before I go out?"

She smiles again and nods feebly. It amazes me still how childlike she can look sometimes.

"No problem," I say. "Don't fall back asleep and leave the taps on though."

I remember to add a smile back at her, so she knows that I am playing with her and not judging her. Of course, I *am* judging her, it's just the kind of stupid thing that she would do.

"Okay, Bun Bun. I'm getting up now. Five minutes."

I nod. "I'll text you in ten to make sure, if you like?"

"I don't need the reminder, but text me anyway," she says, still happy, so at least I haven't fucked it up yet today. "I'll come out with you later, though. We can have a walk together, the three of us."

"Sure," I say. I want to add that it makes no sense to bath now and go out into the woods and get dirty later, but that's how arguments start, so I swallow my words and replace them with another smile.

I don't make the same mistake twice, so I clip Dexter's lead to his collar before we go out. He tugs ahead anyway, dragging me on with him.

"Easy, lad," I say.

Normally I might be tempted to keep pace with him, but with the snare on the first day and the...whatever happened yesterday, I want to be a little more cautious at least.

He looks back at me with what I can only take to be disappointment.

"Don't want you getting over excited again, eh?"

I probably talk to him too much when it's just me and him. I know he can't reply, but he probably understands a lot more than I think he does.

We follow the route that is becoming familiar to me now. He sticks to the path, leading the way, but not trying to tug me off course.

My thoughts are elsewhere.

Eventually, I see it. I thought I would have to search it out, but here it is, crossing the path and running off each way into the pine carpet. Exactly the same as the line by the badger, as the line I saw yesterday, as the line I saw on Monday evening.

"Dex. Dex, sit."

He obeys, and looks at me, his brown eyes quizzical.

I get down and study the dust again. It's ash, grey powdery ash, I'm almost sure of it. I have absolutely no idea why it would be here.

"Weird," I say out loud. I turn to Dex and repeat the word. "Weird."

I haven't come up with any theories between when I first noticed this line and now. To be honest, I have been somewhat preoccupied with other things, but even if I hadn't been, I still don't think I would have any idea.

I get back up to my feet and look off to the left, the same direction that we headed yesterday after the mysterious disturbance, and then to the right. The excitement seems more likely to be to the left, so that's the way I walk. Dexter doesn't argue against it, so we are finally about to find out what this line is, or at least, where it goes.

Dex is trotting along quite happily. He doesn't seem at all twitchy or nervous today. I thought he might pick up the scent of whatever it was that he was after yesterday, but perhaps I have seen too many movies where dogs lead detectives off to solve mysteries. I'm happy that he is calm. That's enough for me.

The line on the ground leads off into the thicker woods, and we follow. It's patchier now: little parts of the line showing, and then a break as it is lost to the leaves. If someone put this here, and surely they must have, they don't do a very good job of maintaining it. Maybe it used to have a purpose and it's not needed anymore. I can't think of any rational explanation for anyone ever needing to form something like this though. A border, maybe? But we are in the woods, on Blackheath's estate. He owns everything out here, as he told us. I look both ways, there doesn't appear to be any distinct difference between the land on either side. A border doesn't make sense.

I've stopped, and Dex is pulling me onwards, straining at his lead. I know he wants to be free, that he wants me to unclip the lead and let him run, but after the last couple of times, I really can't risk it.

"Sorry, boy," I say, and pat him gently on the flank. "Too dangerous here."

As far as I can see, before us and behind, off to either side, all of this is part of the Blackheath Estate. I haven't seen a single other person out here since we arrived. Perhaps Annabel and her daughter were the last people to dare come onto his land. Didn't end too well for them. I shake my head. Guests must visit the cabin all the time. It's a business, a tourist business. Surely he has people in there every week.

We arrived Monday. He probably had a weekend let before us. The cleaners come in when the last guests leave, tidy round, change the linen, leave bread and milk, butter, scones, all those lovely, homely touches. As soon as we have gone, they'll be in mopping up behind us. Saturday morning, ten o'clock, we'll be out of bed, out of the cabin and they will be preparing it for someone else. This week is a temporary stop. We are part of a chain of visitors. Blackheath probably doesn't even remember our names, why would he need to?

Perhaps this line is part of something he has got planned. A marker for a fence he's going to build, or a wall even. Keep the tourists in the cabin, off the main part of his land. That makes sense. Why else would you go to the trouble of marking something out like this?

It's old though. The line is old.

I pause again, wipe aside some pine needles and beige branch parts. It's there, under the debris, it's there. Planned but not completed then. Waiting for the right time? The off season? But it's February. This must be as close to the off-season as you can get. Too early for sun-seekers, too late for a romantic Christmas or New Year getaway. I kick gently at the line of powdery dust, and we move ahead, following it further and further.

Five minutes on, or perhaps closer to ten, Dexter starts to tug on his lead.

"Woah, woah." I pull him back, as gently as I can, and lean down to talk to him. "You okay?"

We're near the place that he was going nuts yesterday. I recognise the slope of the land, the little clearing off in the distance. That's what he is pulling towards.

"What is it?"

There's nothing there. Nothing to see. He must sense something though. The light is filtering through the trees, illuminating the earth in the open area. The ground is speckled with the dappled glow. Katie would love this. I don't want to bring her back to this area, not after yesterday, but she would love it. I take out my phone, and capture the moment for her, taking a photo of the view. These things never come out as well on camera as they look in reality, but it's an approximation of how pretty the scene looks.

I don't think it's the aesthetically appealing view that's making Dexter strain at the lead.

"No," I say. "No. Calm down. Calm down, Dex."

He's trying to drag me. Before I put the phone away, I check the time. We have been out for an hour already. I know that Katie told me to take my time, but I want to be able to spend the day with her. I can't be out here all day. I want to follow the line; I want to know where it goes. I don't have time to follow Dexter as well.

He pulls again, one more time, and yanks his lead free of my hand.

I had the loop around my left hand, gripped tight, and the leather burns my skin as I release it.

"Shit! Dexter! Shit! Come back!" But he's off running out to the clearing, and I'm rubbing my hand against my jeans, trying to combat the deep, searing pain. The skin isn't torn, but, shit, it hurts so much. How did he manage that? I guess he was more determined that I thought.

I have to run after him, of course. My eyes are scanning the ground, looking out for anything that I might fall over, but also scouring the floor for any other animal traps that might harm either of us.

"Dexter!" I shout his name, but he doesn't turn back.

He's racing on. When he gets to the clearing, he stops, stands still, and barks. Barks and barks and barks.

"Stop that! Dexter! Stop!"

Shouting and shouting and barking and barking. I hope Blackheath doesn't call us up to complain about the noise we are making. No wonder he wants to build a fence to keep the rabble away from his home. How far is that from here?

I catch up with Dex, and pick up the loop of his lead, in my other hand this time.

"Don't do that again," I say, in my most stern, assertive tone. "You hurt me." He doesn't understand, and even if he does it doesn't stop him from barking. "Dex, please. Now. Shut up. Stop it. There's nothing here."

I'm walking in a circle around him, looking out into every direction. There are birds in the trees, sure, but he's not looking upwards. He's looking downwards.

"Rabbit? Rat?"

I don't know why I bother asking. I can't see anything, and if he could, he has lost it now. Whatever it was has gone. There's nothing here now apart from him and I. Us two and the trees. The beige carpet, the sunbeam sparkle. That's all there is.

"Let's get on our way," I tell him. "Let's go."

I'm sure there's nothing here, and he's sure that something is. There's no way of breaking the impasse, so I'm going to agree to disagree with him.

"Come on."

It's my turn to tug on the lead now. I pull encouragingly, and he gives one last bark into the empty space between us.

"I don't think we'll come this way again. Come on, Dex."

As we get back to the line, Dexter reluctant but obedient, I look over to the area again. It's quite a distance through the trees, but I can see the sunlight patch. I know that's where it is, and I know that there is nothing there. Something has spooked him, not once but twice. Part of me is glad that I didn't find out what it was.

I get my phone out again before we set off. I forgot to text Katie to make sure she got into the bath. It's probably run out all over the bathroom floor and that means we will get a huge bill from Blackheath. It's way too late to message her, but still, I feel like I should.

Did you get up? How's the bath?

I press send.

I think and send the photograph that I took of the glade as an afterthought.

My phone makes a disappointing bleep, and a message flashes up on my screen

Message not sent

I have no phone signal. Why did I think I would out here in the woods? I take too much for granted living in town, never being far from Wi-Fi never mind a phone signal.

I tell myself that it will be fine, that I always underestimate Katie, and I try to make myself believe it.

Dexter keeps looking over his shoulder back to the clearing too, but he hasn't made any more moves to race off. My left hand is still throbbing, I don't think I could bear the same happening to my right.

It's for the best if we move along, and probably for the best if I don't bring him back here.

"You're a town dog, aren't you? Parks and footpaths, not dirt tracks and woods, eh?"

He knows I am talking to him, and he wags his tail. That's better, that's what we want.

Back on the line, I have to check behind, the way we originally came, to see where to move onwards. There isn't much trace of it here without sweeping the leaves out of the way.

I could just let this go, and head back to Katie now, but it is niggling away at me.

Sometimes when I'm playing poker I get into some spots. Like, I feel like I'm betting my winning hand, playing a strong game, and then – boom! We get to the last card, I think I've got the other player right where I want them, but as soon as I make a bet, they raise me, and it turns the whole hand around. I have to make a decision about whether to call or fold. The thing is, if you fold, well, you never know if they had you beat or if they were bluffing. One thing I hate, that I absolutely hate, is not knowing. I'll be in the tank, working through the hand, thinking out each move we both made, trying to reason through it, trying to focus. I know that I shouldn't say anything, and if they have any sense that they won't say anything that might help me to get a read, but I always want to ask whether they will show me what they have if I fold. I can't bear not knowing. I feel the same about this line. It's got into my head. I have to know why the hell I keep seeing it, and where it goes.

Katie said for us to take our time, and I want this time. I want some man and dog time with Dex. I want to explore and adventure and be a big kid for a while. She's doing her girlie thing, pampering and preening and all that shit. This is fine. This is all fine.

We press on, Dex walking ahead, stopping every now and again to sniff something he finds interesting, and taking more leaks that I thought possible for one average-sized Labrador with what I assume is an average-sized bladder. Despite thinking that we have as much time as I want to take, it seems to take inordinately long for us to reach exactly where I thought we would: the remains of the badger. There's just a gross furry pile here, the actual mass of body has gone, what is left behind is thick sticky dirty red mush.

Dex moves in before I can pull him back, sniffing and investigating.

"No! Stop that. Jeez, Dexter."

I yank him away, and he looks up in disappointment. Finally, something interesting for him to see and I stop him. I can imagine what he must be thinking. I walk him on, across the road track.

We started out on the other side of the cabin, and we have looped around, through the woods to this point. A quick calculation tells me that the line that we have followed so far forms a semicircle, with the cabin in roughly the centre. Perhaps the cabin is exactly in the centre. My early idea about a boundary fence seems to fit in with this deduction. Someone marked out where a fence would go. Across the track though? A gate maybe. An entry point for tourists or visitors to the cabin.

I want to keep going, to head onwards, follow the line to complete what I assume is full circle. I have snippets of information, and I have to make a logical deduction from them, just like when I'm in a hand of poker. I never know everything I need to know, because I can't see the other players' hands. Now, without carrying on along the line, I can't know for sure that it will complete the circuit. Still, I'm almost sure it does. Keep walking, or head back to Katie? I know what I want to do, but instead, I pull Dexter to heel and we head along the track, back towards the cabin.

Chapter Ten

Something's not right.

We reach the front of the cabin, and Dex races for the door, presses his nose against it and pushes it open. I know that I locked it when we went out, and I don't expect Katie would have bothered to go out without us. I remember that I underestimate her most of the time and try to keep myself in check.

"Katie," I call. I stand outside and wait to hear her reply.

Perhaps she slipped out around the back of the cabin. I make the snap decision to look around before I go in. I walk around the side of the house, and I half expect to find her on the bench at the rear as I walk around the corner, but it is empty. She's not out here.

"Katie!" I shout louder. No answer.

"Okay," I say to myself, and head back to the door. Maybe she got some fresh air, went back indoors, forgot to click the door shut properly and I'm out here getting all anxious about nothing.

As I enter, I nearly trip over Dex, who was on his way back out to me.

"Where's Katie? You find her?"

He barks, one short sharp word of a noise that I don't understand.

Something's definitely not right.

The lounge is empty. The sofa and armchair are still as we left them when we went to bed, as far as I can tell. The fireguard is in front of the wood burner, everything looks in order. Her sensible shoes, the only flat, comfortable outdoorsy pair she has were muddy, next to the door on the hessian mat. They aren't there now. Her jacket was on the peg behind the entrance too, and that's also missing.

"Katie!" I call again, and again there's no response.

I hurry through to the kitchen. Empty coffee cup and side plate on the dish drainer. She's had breakfast and washed up after herself. She definitely got out of bed then. As I can't see a pool of water coming from the bathroom and I don't hear the taps I think it's fair to assume she got her bath.

I have a terrible sickening feeling in my gut. An image flashes into my mind of her lying in the tub, facemask on, bubbles everywhere, super-relaxed, falling asleep, slipping under the water.

"Katie. Katie. Katie." My voice gets louder with each time I repeat her name, as I race to the bathroom.

The bath is empty. No Katie. No bathwater. Nothing. The bath towel is hanging on the radiator now, so she did have a bath. Did she? I press my hand against it. Yes, it's damp. She had a bath.

Dexter is following me around, and I don't notice him as I turn to leave the room and almost trip over him.

"Go and lie down." My voice is too harsh. I don't mean to shout at him, but my stress transfers to my voice, and he gets the end result of that directed at him.

He trots off to the living room with his head and tail drooping despondently.

I take a breath before I push the bedroom door open. I want to see her lying there, maybe naked or semi-naked on the bed, pulling some prank on me, laughing at the look on my face as I see her. I want her to have lain back on the bed and fallen asleep. I want her to be in the room.

She is not.

The room is empty.

So, where the hell has she gone?

No one is ever out of reach these days of course. I stop stressing for a moment to pull my phone out of my pocket and call her. So simple.

I click the green phone button, and nothing happens.

I click again. Nothing.

I have no phone signal. Still. Even here in the cabin.

I know for certain that I could access internet here on Tuesday night when I was searching for information about that missing girl. Internet access does not always mean there is a phone signal though. Have I texted anyone since I have been here? The only person I ever really message is Katie, and I have been with her pretty much all the time.

No problem. Don't worry. If I have internet, I can send her a message through an app. We have at least three apps installed that I can use to call or message her. I've not used them before, I've never had to, but I know that I can, and they can't be all that difficult.

I'm not a Facebook fan, but I have Messenger installed, and I click onto the chat log showing the few communications I have had with Katie. It's mostly a list of her sending me links to posts that she thinks I will find amusing. Dogs, cartoons, cartoons about dogs, you get the picture. I see the little phone signal at the top of the page and click.

Couldn't make call. You need to be connected to your network or Wi-Fi to make calls

No Wi-Fi? No internet? I can't remember the last time I was without any kind of network connection. It's a strange sensation. I feel incredibly vulnerable and detached, and I have no idea how I can get in touch with Katie.

My stupid brain tries to suggest that I call Roman Blackheath to complain about the lack of internet. I shut it up immediately.

So, Katie isn't here, and I have no way of contacting her. I guess I should make some food, sort Dexter out, and wait. What else can I do?

But the door was unlocked.

I screw my eyes up and think about it for a few moments. The door opens inwards. Katie would have had to pull it shut behind her. Perhaps she just got distracted and forgot to tug it closed. She does get distracted. Quite easily in fact. She might have gone to check her phone, gotten annoyed that there was no internet and kept walking without thinking to make sure the cabin was locked. I put pieces of the puzzle together to form a solution. This is something else that I have learned from poker. Poker is a game of incomplete information. As a player you never see the big picture until the hand is over, but you can put together what you know and what you can infer from the information that you have.

How did someone behave when they saw their cards? How do they respond to your bets, or how do they act? What do they say? What do they not say? Has the fat man just received his food order and yet he's leaving his greasy burger and cheesy fries the side table to play this hand against you, the first hand he has played in half an hour, despite his crappy meal going cold? That's a man you don't want to mess with. That man has a decent hand. Incomplete information, but clues. Clues everywhere. I piece together what I know.

All I am certain of is that Katie is not here.

I pour a glass of water, and take it through to the living room, where Dex has settled onto the rug. He looks up at me as I sit, and I stroke his head. He forgives me so easily when I shout at him, but I still try not to do it too often. I guess you could say that he and Katie are the same in many ways.

I try to sip at the water slowly; I try to stay calm. Sit and wait, I tell myself, sit and wait.

Then it hits me. The bedroom. It's not what wasn't there that matters, it's what was there. Katie was clearly absent, but on the table. Beside the bed. I'm sure I saw it. It didn't register in my stupid brain at first, but sitting here, thinking back over the details, I'm sure it is there.

I leap to my feet, and Dexter scrambles to stand up too. He has this dazed, confused look on his face, but he follows faithfully anyway.

I race down the corridor, and slam through the door into the bedroom.

I was right.

On the table, next to the bed.

It's there.

Katie's necklace. The pendant she only ever takes off to sleep or to bath or shower.

It's there.

The pendant she would never leave behind, in a home that isn't our home, unlocked, unsecured. She would not have left this here by choice. Something has happened.

I get my phone out again, just in case, but there's still no signal. No network, no internet, nothing.

I pick up the necklace, feeling the weight of the ash-filled crucifix in the palm of my hand. The casket is the heavy part, not the ashes inside it. As soon as I think of the word "ashes" my mind flicks straight to the circle around the cabin.

There's something I'm missing, but I don't know what it is.

I stuff the necklace into my jeans pocket, and, Dexter chasing behind, I race back along the corridor and out of the door.

Chapter Eleven

I have no idea where to begin. I have a brief moment's thought of getting Dexter to track her down, sniff the ground and work out which way she went. That's how this would go in a movie. I'd wave an item of her clothing under his nose, and he would rush off in her direction. Or he would know her scent so well that he wouldn't even need to smell anything first, he would drop his nose to the floor and be hot on her heels, no problem. As it is, Dexter is wagging his tail frantically, circling me in confusion.

"Okay," I say. "Okay." I'm trying to think, trying to make a plan. "Think. Think." I put my hands on my knees in a chair squat, working out what to do.

I can't phone anyone. I can't contact anyone. I could get in the car and drive on up to Blackheath's house, or back down to the main road, along, try to find the entrance to his drive. We didn't see it when I missed the turning that first day. Maybe there's a different route I need to take. What would I say? He must have a landline; he must have internet. If I find out how to get to his house he can help, or at least help me to get help.

That's one plan.

The thing is, I don't want to drive away and not even try to look for Katie first. Despite my feelings that something sinister must be happening, I could be totally overreacting. She wouldn't leave the cabin without me, and she would never leave without her necklace. I have to go after her. Plan A is finding Katie. Plan B is finding Roman and getting help.

Dex sits in front of me and looks up at me in agreement.

"Let's go find Katie," I tell him.

I still have no idea where to begin.

We started our walk earlier to the left of the cabin: straight ahead until we came to the circle and then anti-clockwise around the loop until we arrived back here. Unless Katie somehow managed to stay behind us all the way, the balance of probability suggests that she can't be in the area that we last walked through. If she'd come out of the house in the last ten to fifteen minutes and she was on the track between badger and cabin, we would have seen her.

If she were being taken somewhere she didn't want to go I'm pretty sure we would have heard her. Unless she was unable to make any noise. Unless she was…I don't want to think about any of the things that might have happened to her. I can't think that way. I make a decision. I'm going to walk back along the same route we took this morning, in the same direction, or at least that's my opening bet.

We walk to the left of the cabin and through the break in the trees that is becoming so familiar now. On the first evening here, I was filled with excitement for the countryside and trepidation for our relationship. Now I feel like that has been flipped on its head. I'm actually afraid of what is going on here, and I had finally started to be optimistic about our relationship. Especially after Katie started to open up about her mum last night; I really felt like we were getting somewhere. Now this. It doesn't make sense.

Dex tugs me onwards. He knows where he is going now, or at least he thinks he does.

Despite having written him off as a tracker dog, I call down to him. "Where's Katie? Find Katie, Dex."

You never know, perhaps I am underestimating him, in the same way I have always underestimated Katie. He wags his tail again, but shows no sign of having any hidden abilities that I haven't discovered. At least I tried.

I try to keep my thoughts in check as we head onwards. I'm fairly certain that if there were any more snares out here, we would have found them this morning or on one of our other walks this week. The trap that snagged Dexter's leg must have been a one off, a remnant, forgotten. Still, I'm careful to look at the ground as we head on, not quite breaking a jog.

"Katie!"

I keep shouting her name, hoping that I will hear her reply, her voice sounding out from behind a tree or through the bushes. Every time I call, I'm met with only silence.

I look off to either side of the path, trying to identify any sign of movement, looking for clues. I don't know enough about tracking to pick out where she might have walked. I know someone more experienced or more skilled that I am might be able to look at the way a twig has been snapped, or a shrub has been disturbed, and know that this must be the way that she passed, but I have people-reading skills not plant-reading skills. My abilities are useless here. There are no footprints that I can follow, not even from my own trek earlier. No doubt I'd have ended up following my own path anyway.

Perhaps I should have driven to Blackheath's house. I could have found the way. It can't be that difficult. Then a thought hits me. When we arrived on Monday, he didn't have a car with him. He hadn't driven to meet us. Perhaps the quickest way from the cabin to his house is on foot. I know the general direction of the manor, so perhaps instead of walking around the loop I should walk straight down there to find him and get help. I have been out here looking for her, I have made an attempt to carry out Plan A. I'm going to carry on to the manor and get help.

I can already imagine Roman telling me to calm down and go back and wait for her. I don't know how to explain this feeling of unease to myself, so how will I explain it to him? I'm happy with my decision though. I feel like this is the right thing to do. If Katie is nearby, she will hear me. If not, then I think I am going to need more help. Or to be reassured that I should chill out.

Onwards, trying not to think, shouting Katie's name, looking in every direction, seeing nothing but trees, trees, trees.

We pass the powder line, the ashes, and keep going, onwards, on a path we have never taken until now. This route has been trodden before; it seems to add up that this is the way that Blackheath and his workers must come to the cabin. Perhaps the cleaners and caretakers only come by car, straight to the cabin and never walk this way, maybe it is only Blackheath that treads this line, but either way, it is here, and I am sure this must be the right direction. I wonder why he hasn't placed lights along the route if he travels this way at night, but there are already enough questions buzzing around my head for me to quickly disregard another.

Onwards. Onwards again. Dex stops abruptly in front of me and I almost run into him. In fact I do run into him, the almost part is that I just about manage to stop myself from tripping over him and ending up flat on my face amongst the dead pine debris.

"Thanks, buddy." I mutter the words, keeping my voice down, looking all around us, trying to see what it is that he has seen.

"What is it?"

He's sniffing at the air, turning his head. He has a look of curiosity rather than fear. His fur isn't fluffed up with adrenaline this time. He's picked up on something though, so I let him go with it.

His nose twitches as he samples the scent. I wish I had this superpower. I wish I could pick up on traces of Katie's expensive, pungent bath bomb fragrance, track her and take her home. All I can smell is woodland. It's not the pine essence of air freshener or the candles that Katie buys at Christmas time, no. The real pine trees in the forest smell dry, dusty, and green. Green isn't officially a smell, of course, but that earthy nature stench can't be called anything else.

For a minute Dex remains steadfastly still, and I let him take his time, hoping that he will piece together the information that he is processing, in much the way that I do. I stand by his side, silent, trying not to distract him from his calculations. Eventually, he looks up and me, looks back to the track and starts walking.

I can't be sure whether we are just heading forwards in the same way that we would have been if he had never paused for thought, or if we are on the trail of something or someone. I let him lead me along, and I stay as alert as I can.

We haven't walked much further before I hear a scuffling sound in between the trees. I pull Dexter to another stop, put my finger to my lips and say, "Ssh," as quietly as I can manage whilst still being heard by the dog.

I duck down a little into an uncomfortable half-crouch and look in the direction of the noise.

Again, I hear it, a rustling. This time, Dexter has caught up with what's happening, and he angles his entire body in the direction of the noise, poised for action.

"Ssh," I say again.

I can't see anything. The noise seems to be coming from close to one of the trunks. There's no way a person could hide behind there and not be visible, and as I finally see the small grey body of a squirrel scurrying across and up towards the branches, I let out a disappointed moan.

Dex jumps up at me, placing his front paws onto my chest, splattering me with dirt from the woodland floor and tries to lick at my face. I'd usually yell at him, but instead I lean forwards so that he can deliver his sloppy dog kiss. I need this right now. I need him. I can feel my heart pounding, I can almost hear it. I have to find Katie. I know she must be in trouble. I know it. We have wasted so much time, she and I. If I had known that all I had to do was to get her to open up about her mother, we could have started to put things right between us a long time ago. Was that all it was though, or was that loss, her pain, only a contributing factor to the decaying of our relationship?

It was only after she lost her mother that we bought Dexter. I thought that she needed something else to channel her love towards. What I really should have done was to spend time with her, to listen to her, to help her. Instead, we got Dex. I panicked, to be honest. I was scared that the replacement that she might want would be a baby, and there was no way that I was ready for that. I'm still not. Not now, and maybe not ever.

In poker we have something called a blocker-bet. It's a small bet that you make when you don't really want the other player to make a *big* bet and put you in a difficult position. You might think that your hand is okay, but not particularly brilliant. You might think that if your opponent makes a huge bet, you're going to be left facing a situation you don't want to be in. You make a blocker bet in the hope that they will just call instead of raising the stakes. Dexter was my blocker bet. I offered to get a dog so that she didn't ask me to have a baby with her. Thinking of life in terms of poker can be helpful. It's not helping me much right now.

When she was about to turn thirty last year, Katie became obsessed with the idea of getting married. To me, of course. I don't know what it is about that milestone. Who perpetuated the idea that women should be married before thirty? They should be locked up. She asked me over and over, and I stalled, and made excuses. The excuses were in fact solid reasons why two people who are having quite a difficult relationship probably shouldn't get married, but Katie didn't see things my way. If we got married, things would get better, she told me. It seemed ridiculous, and it still does. Someone chose this arbitrary age and raised women's expectations of themselves and how their lives should be. I can see now that really all we ever needed was to communicate better, to spend time together and relax. There has been so much tension, so much stress between us, we haven't stood a chance. I'm not ready to get married and have a baby with Katie, still I'm not, but I do want her back safely. I do want to spend my future with her. I know that now. I know that.

I have to find her.

We are completely lost. We must be. Somehow, we've walked around in a circle. I don't understand it. There's no way that we could have looped back on ourselves, walking in a straight line away from the cabin. No way, but somehow that is exactly what must have happened. Beneath my feet on the path is the line of ash.

"What the hell?"

Dexter looks at me, and I look at him, sharing a look of confusion. I'm confused about how this has happened and he is confused about what is wrong with me.

"How did we do this, Dex? How the…"

And then I realise.

I look around us, taking everything in, thinking, thinking, thinking.

It *isn't* possible for us to have gone in a circle. We haven't. This is a different line.

"What the absolute hell?"

I kneel and touch the dust. It's exactly the same as the other line, but we are far deeper into the woods, much closer to Blackheath's manor. There's a line around his house then? He was going to build two fences? I suppose that's possible. If you are hiring someone to come out, then why not kill two fences with one stone, or two birds with one fence builder? As with the other line, I check in each direction and this too runs off both ways.

"Well…whatever," I say to Dex, and he takes the opportunity to lick me again. "Hey, hey!" I laugh and try to settle him just as he lets out an almighty meaty bark right into my face.

"Dexter!"

He barks again. And again. And again. He's looking past me off to the left and into the woods.

"I guess you've seen something more exciting this time. Let's go."

I feel a little safer with Dexter than I would on my own, but I still feel a ripple of fear as we head off the path and into the trees.

He's still barking as we walk, and I don't know whether I should quiet him or not. We've lost the element of surprise anyway, so maybe it's best to let him carry on. If it is Katie, she will hear him. If it's anything dangerous, perhaps the barking will see it off.

There's nothing dangerous, I remind myself. Nothing to fear out here.

Then I see her.

It's Katie.

In the distance, just wandering between the trees. She looks like she is on drugs or sleepwalking, weaving in and out. What is she doing? I shake my head.

"Dexter. She's there. Okay. Calm down now. Everything's okay."

He's still pulling at the lead, and when he sees what I've seen he snaps forward, ripping the loop from my hand again.

I should have learned after last time, because now, the leather rips through my palm and grazes the top layer of my skin. If I thought the pain burned before, I didn't know how lightly I had been let off. I crunch over in a ball of pain and pull my hand in to my body.

"Dexter, you asshole! Come back! Katie! Katie! Wait!"

I riffle through my pocket for a handkerchief or a tissue or anything that I can wrap around my hand, but I have nothing. My fingers make contact with Katie's crucifix, the smooth silver has been warmed by its proximity to my leg and my body heat.

I stretch and contract my left hand, the one that is searingly painful. I need to start wearing gloves, or I need to not bring Dexter to places like this.

In the distance, I can see that Dexter has almost caught up with Katie.

She's started to run. At first my brain thinks that she's seen him and is running towards him, but it only takes a few seconds for me to realise that I am misinterpreting what I see.

She is running away.

I turn my head, looking across the landscape, trying to work out what she is running from.

"Katie!" I yell again, and she seems to pause, only slightly, before continuing to flee.

She must have seen Dex. She must have seen me. Why is she going in the opposite direction?

I get closer, and I hear her.

"Help me. Help me. Help."

She is hollering the words, running and screaming, and I pick up my pace to get to her as quickly as I can.

Suddenly she comes to an abrupt stop, like a racehorse pulling up at a fence. I see it clearly. Dexter is almost next to her. She stands still, just for a flicker, and I see her look at the ground, before she turns on her heels and runs off in another direction.

What did she see? What the hell is happening here?

I shout her name. "It's okay. I'm coming. Stay where you are. I'm nearly there."

She's fast. I didn't realise she was this quick. Underestimating her again, I suppose. I still can't see what it is she is running from.

"Leave me alone. You need to go. Get out of here. Get away."

"It's me, Katie. It's me!"

She must know that it's me, because Dexter is at her feet now. I hear a blood-chilling yelp from him. Has he stepped into another snare? Has someone got hold of him? Oh no, no. She is kicking him. He has caught up to her and she has kicked him, square in the belly.

"Dexter. Dexter come here," I shout. I have no idea what is going on anymore.

"Katie! What are you doing? Katie, stop. Stop." I'm almost screaming.

Dexter has stopped running, he's standing still, probably as confused as I am. I'm soon level with him.

"I'll come back in a minute, Dex. Stay there, stay."

I keep running, running, shouting and running, until I catch up with Katie.

I'm right behind her.

She doesn't turn around; she doesn't look at me.

Have I done something wrong again? I try to think quickly, reel through the events of the morning, checking every word I said, every action I made. Did I do something that inadvertently upset her? It's difficult to know sometimes, sure, but I really can't think of anything this time. Did I leave something lying around? I'm not coming up with any explanation.

"Katie," I say again.

She keeps walking.

"Katie, stop!"

I reach her, put my hand on her shoulder, and

Chapter Twelve

My head hurts. That's the first thing I think, and it's a powerful thought. My head really hurts. Everything is a blur. It's not like a hangover, not that kind of grogginess. It's not like coming around from anaesthetic. It's like the seconds before you fall asleep. That in-between time, when nothing is quite…I want to say nothing is quite real, but that's not it. It's like when you're in the sea, treading water, and you think you can put your feet down and they'll be on the sand below, but then you try, and there's nothing. You're too far out. You look back at the beach and you've drifted further than you meant to. Your heart skips, your pulse is all over the place, your mind floods with desperation. You're lost. Truly all at sea. I have that split-second panic-fear-confusion cocktail, and it lasts for longer than that split-second.

It's light, but not bright. It's light but not daylight. It's light, there's a light, a bulb, hanging, dangling, distant. Not so distant. Two metres? One?

There's sound. A voice. Two voices. Three. A man. A woman. Two voices. No. I'm speaking. The third voice is mine. I barely recognise it. I feel the words forming in my mouth, floating into the room.

It's cold. I'm cold. My jacket. I don't have my jacket. I was…where was I? What was I doing? I had my jeans, my shirt, my jumper. Where's my jumper? My phone. I had my phone. I try to get my hand to reach to my pocket, underneath me, to the back of my jeans, but it won't move. It resists. I try again, but no. Look down. Everything is a blur. My thoughts circle, spiral, cycle. Look down. Focus. Try to focus. My hands are…I'm on a chair. A wooden chair. I know because the arms are wooden, shiny, clean polished mahogany. Nice chair. Looks expensive. My hands are…there's rope, some kind of dirty grey rope. Rope around my wrists, rope around the arms of the chair.

Focus. Focus, Seb. Focus. Where's Dexter? I was with Dex. We were…

"He's bad. Your dog. He's a bad dog." Her voice is dry.

"Sorry…what?" My vision is fading in and out of blackness. "What did you say? Who are you? Where am I?"

"Not so many questions." The man's voice.

"Your dog tried to chase me out of the circle. He's a bad dog. He nearly made me go over the line." The girl.

She sounds young, very young, but I think she must be older than her voice is telling me.

"That's enough," the man says.

"But I…"

"No," he repeats, and the female voice falls silent.

Concentrate. Think. Where am I? What happened?

"You were wandering."

Did I speak out loud? Can he read my mind? Don't be stupid, Seb.

"Seb, is it? Seb. Seb, you are here, with us. That's all you need to know now.

"Where's Dexter?" I know that I am speaking aloud this time. I feel the pain in my face, and taste blood in my mouth.

I try again to look around the room. Whatever they have done, they have done a good job of it. He hit me? They drugged me? Both? Where the hell is Dexter.

"He's a bad boy," the woman says.

She's not a woman, she's a girl. Somewhere on the cusp of girl and woman. I don't know. I don't know anything.

"Seb is a bad boy."

The man sounds like he's definitely the one in control here. Her father? Her…what? Not her husband, partner, boyfriend.

"Yes. I'm in control," he says. "I'm in control here. I'm in control of her, and now I am in control of you."

I need to concentrate. Concentrate.

Everything fades to blackness again.

Blackness. I open my eyes and there is still blackness.

"Hello?" I'm lying down now. On my back, with my hands tied together on my belly. They (he?) must have untied me and tied me again. I was…I was on a chair. I was in the woods. I was with Dexter. I am…Katie is missing. Dexter is missing.

"You are missing, Seb. You are missing."

The room explodes with light. Artificial, bright, glaring light. A strip light, in the middle of the room, above the chair. I'm not in the chair. I'm on a bed. She is on the chair. She is looking at me. Staring at me. She looks…what? What is that look? Curiosity?

She covers her face and I'm sure she is hiding a laugh in her palm. What is there to laugh about? What could anyone find amusing about this situation?

Her face snaps into a serious, flat expression.

"Am I speaking? What the hell have you done to me?"

"Questions, questions."

The man is by my head, standing beside the bed.

The small bed is metal framed, but I haven't been tied to it. My hands are bound together, but I could get to my feet, and get out of here if I tried. I could...

"Seb." A hand presses onto my chest, and a burst of pain rips through me. "You need to stop talking."

I do.

"You do."

The girl laughs; she actually laughs.

I want to get up, I want to get out of here. I don't even know where I am.

"I am missing. That's what you said, before. I'm missing."

I see the movement of the man's head as he nods.

"You are. I'm afraid that once you saw..." he gestures towards the girl. "Her. Well, I had to stop you. We couldn't have you going telling everyone."

"She's not a ghost."

Her face is translucent pale. Her hair dark, long, held in an untidy plait. She could be a ghost.

"No, Seb. Of course, she's not a ghost."

The girl laughs again. It's a shrill, high-pitched childish chirp of a laugh. It sounds strangely innocent considering the circumstances.

"I'm not a ghost."

"Very good," the man says to her, his voice flat and emotionless.

He sounds bored. If there's one thing I am definitely not, right now, it is bored.

"Who are you, and what the hell is going on?"

He moves his face closer to mine, and he looks somehow familiar. I've never seen him before but there's something about him that I recognise.

"I am Roman Blackheath."

If there's one thing I'm sure of, it's that this man is not the same man who greeted me and Katie on Monday evening. That man was younger, shorter. That man was a completely different person.

"You look even more confused now." Everything he says elicits laughter from the girl. She's loving this for some bizarre reason. "I'm not surprised. No. Not at all. It must all be very strange to you. Not used to having to think much, are you?"

I concentrate, make sure I'm only thinking my thoughts, not speaking aloud. Much as I underestimate Katie, this man is underestimating me. I think a lot. My whole job is built around thinking, working things out, making the right decisions. Blackheath regards me cautiously. I've been saying too much, and now I'm saying too little.

"You're starting to think. You are, aren't you? I can almost hear the effort you're putting in. Well done. Well done, Seb."

The girl claps her hands. There's something not right about her.

"Am I…are we in your house?" If we are, we are in some run-down back room. The space is around twenty feet by twenty feet. There's this bed, the chair and another chair like it, which Roman is choosing not to use. Along the far wall there are a bookcase and a wardrobe. To the left, a dressing table and mirror. To the right, a bare white space. The furnishing is mismatched and minimal to say the least. It strikes me that there are no windows. The darkness earlier, it wasn't because I'd been unconscious until night-time, but who knows, perhaps I was. Primarily, it was dark because the light was turned off, and there are no windows.

"You are definitely starting to think, aren't you?"

Roman's breath is hot against my face. He's too close, right next to me. He smells like he needs to visit a dentist. His stench is rotten, putrid.

He's right though. I'm starting to think.

"The man who came to welcome us, the keyholder, that wasn't you?"

He waves the idea away with one swipe of his immense hand. "I don't trouble myself with that kind of thing. I have people. I have staff. I don't need to smile at ghastly tourists."

"No, but you want our money. Why else are you renting out the cabin? You must need the money."

"What I want, Mr Archer, is the appearance of normality."

He leaves the sentence hanging in the air, and I try to conceal my confused expression. The appearance of normality?

"And her." I nod my head over to the girl. "Is she one of your staff? What does she do for you?"

"Oh Sebastian. You haven't really started to think at all have you?"

This girl. She must be the one the locals have seen walking in the woods. A stranger, one of Roman's team, an outsider. They weren't expecting to see a girl out here, so they jump to their own conclusions. It's a bit of a stretch, or at least it would be if she weren't so pale and quite frankly rather scary looking.

"That's not very kind," she says. "And I'm not an outsider. I'm not am I? I'm inside most of the time. Outside is dangerous. Once a day. Stay between the lines."

Roman puts a finger to his lips. "Stop talking now. Stop now."

"But he called me a ghost, and then he called me an outsider. He's being mean and I don't like him."

"This is why you stay away from strangers," he walks over to her and gently strokes her hair. "Strangers are bad people. They don't understand how special you are. They don't understand that you need to be protected."

"Special," she repeats the word under her breath, and then carries on repeating it to herself.

"Special, yes."

"Mean dog. Mean man."

"Hush now," Roman snaps, and the girl falls silent.

"Where is Katie?"

"Where is Katie? I thought she would be with us by now. I have someone with her, keeping her busy."

"If you've hurt her, I swear I…"

"It doesn't look like you will be doing very much at all, does it?"

"I will. If you have hurt her, I promise I will."

He smiles and shakes his head.

"I can't let you go now, of course. Now that you have seen her."

"Katie?"

He looks as confused as I feel.

"My girl here. Why do you think I had to bring you down here?"

"Because you're messed up in the head and you lure tourists into your cabin so you can…" I wave my hand around the room in a vague gesture.

"So, I can do what?"

I don't want to think about what he plans to do. Especially if he doesn't intend to let me go. It's clear that I have to work out how to get out of here though.

My mind goes back to an early thought, an earlier realisation. No windows. This room has no windows. More importantly, if I am going to work out how to escape, there are no doors.

Roman sees me looking around, but I'm only half-focussed on my search. What I really want to see is where he looks. I want to pick up a tell from him. If he sees me frantically looking for an exit route, I'd put money on the fact that he will look at the exit. It's a force of habit, doing these little things that give us away. It's locked into our subconscious. Thinking of making a big bet? You're going to look at your chips. Before it's even your turn to act, your brain is planning ahead, you know what you are going to do. If you haven't conditioned yourself to hide your tells and keep that poker face, you can give a lot of information away without even realising. I'm trying to make it look as if I am looking for the door, but I am looking for information.

Roman looks up. I don't follow his line of vision, but now I know. Now I have information. I don't know what I am going to do with that information, but upwards is the way out.

We are underground.

I keep my expression not flat, but just as I think he would expect it to be: mildly panicked.

There's a lot to take in. I need to take a step back.

"Who are you?" I ask the girl.

She looks at Roman, as if for permission to speak. He shakes his head firmly, and he answers instead.

"That is none of your concern."

"But…" I start to speak, and he cuts me off.

"Are you not more interested in the answer to your other question? What am I going to do with you?"

"If you were going to kill me, you'd have done it already, surely?"

An excited look crosses the girl's face. I bare my teeth at her like a cornered animal, and she looks away.

"Mean man."

"The thing is, Seb. I can't have you talking to anyone about my girl here."

I don't understand.

"I don't know anything about her. I've never seen her before. Not before…It was her? In the wood? I thought Dexter had found Katie, but it was her?"

She nods.

Of course, if I hadn't been so busy panicking, I would have worked this out already. She saw Dexter, the mean dog. She said something about the line. The circle.

"What is the circle?"

Roman is about to tell the girl to keep silent when there's a crackling sound and a beep from his pocket.

He walks over to the corner of the room, and speaks into a black, bricklike walkie-talkie. The room is so small that although he is muttering as quietly as he can, I can hear every word he says.

"No. Keep her there. I don't care. No. Can't I trust you to…no…I said keep her there."

He clicks a red button on top of the unit, pressing it forcefully, channelling anger that seems to have come from the conversation he just had.

"Looks like I am going to have to leave you two for a few minutes." He glances at the woman, and then glares at me. My hands are bound together, my legs tied at the ankles. He's done a good job with the knots, or at least I assume it was him.

"Your girlfriend isn't complying with our plan, I am afraid."

"You leave her alone. I tell you, leave her…" but I don't finish my sentence, as Roman crams a cloth handkerchief into my mouth, and looks around for something to secure it in place. He makes do with a stocking hanging out of what I imagine must be the woman's drawers.

The woman's drawer. The woman's bed. I'm slow on the uptake, but I realise, she must live here. In this cellar. In this underground space, this tiny windowless prison. I look at her, I look, and I look. Just as everything starts to make sense the blackness forms around me again.

Chapter Thirteen

I open my eyes and despite still being tied I jump back across the bed. The woman is kneeling next to the side of the bed, her face only centimetres from mine.

"Don't tell!" she shrieks and scuttles back over to the chair.

"What the hell!" I shake my head, trying to wake myself up, snap back to full consciousness. The gag is no longer in my mouth then. He drugged me? On the cloth? Did she…?

"Did you take the gag out?" I ask her. She looks confused. "The cloth in my mouth. Did you take it out?" And now she looks scared.

"Don't tell. Please. Don't tell. I wanted to talk to you. I…" She puts her finger onto her own lips, sealing them shut.

I remember what I was thinking before Roman left.

"Do you live here? Is this your room?"

She looks around, as if looking for Blackheath. Now she has no one to ask for permission. I can almost smell her uncertainty.

"He said I shouldn't talk to you." She puts her finger back onto her lips, and then almost immediately removes it again. "I don't have anyone to talk to though. I'm not allowed to talk to people." Her voice, below that layer of childlike tone, is rasping and I can tell that she is speaking the truth. Her voice sounds hardly used.

"You can just nod or shake your head if you want to. That's not talking, is it?"

She thinks about this, turning her head one way and then the other, as though tossing the idea about in her mind. Finally, she looks at me and nods.

"Okay, good." I smile, trying to look as friendly as possible. "So, do you live here? Is this your room?"

As I expected she would, she nods.

This is messed up. Why is this girl living down here in Blackheath's cellar?

My mind starts to focus. Why am I wasting my time trying to work out who she is and why she is here? I should be thinking about getting the hell out.

Now Blackheath has gone, I can check out the ceiling without alerting him. Above the far corner of the room is a square that looks different to the rest of the dirty, white-painted area around it. I can see the tracings of the outline of an opening. That must be it. The exit. But how do I get up there? How did Roman get up there? How do I get out?

The steps must be on the other side, folded on top of a trapdoor, maybe? If I open the door, I can pull them down. Push up on the hatch and loop them through somehow.

"You can't go up there."

She is watching me, never taking her eyes off me. I'm hardly concealing what it is that I'm planning.

"You're not meant to speak," I remind her.

She shakes her head, folds her lips inward, clamps them shut. Then she points up at the hatch and shakes her head again.

"I get it," I say. "I can't go up there. But up there is the whole world, and down here is, well, down here is a little room that I don't intend on staying in for the rest of my life. And if Roman Blackheath is planning on making sure the rest of my life isn't very long at all, I need to get out of here, so, I'm sorry if I can't go up there, but I *am* going to."

She lets out an immense, fierce scream.

"Shut up, shut up, shut UP!" I bark.

The last thing I want is Blackheath coming back down here before I've even made a plan, never mind worked out how to put it into practice.

She does not shut up.

This enclosed, nasty hole is not made any better by having to share it with a wailing banshee.

"Ghost…" I say, remembering what she said earlier. "You're not a ghost."

This stops her. I thought it would get her attention.

"Why do people think you are a ghost?" I ask, tentatively.

She thrashes her head from side to side this time.

"It's okay. You can talk now. You *are* allowed. I promise."

I shuffle myself into a sitting position, arduously swinging my legs onto the floor. It's hard work, but I want to be eye-to-eye with her. I want to look at her properly, and I do. I stare, and I know that I am making her uncomfortable, but I have to do this.

She stays silent.

She is, as I first estimated, a young woman. It's difficult to age her, due to her pearlescent white skin, which is clear and remarkably free of blemishes considering the fact she appears to live in a small underground room. Her hair is wild and uncared for, tied into a childlike plait, but she is far from being a child. Childish in nature, sure, but there's something going on behind those eyes. She must be around twenty years old or thereabouts. I figure there is no point asking her. What I do know is that this is not the ghost of Annabel Harford.

And that's when it hits me. She is. She is Annabel's ghost. Audrey was three-years-old eighteen years ago, she would be twenty-one now. She would be the same age as this girl. The dark hair, that face. The photos on the internet news reports. She can't be. She can't have been here all this time. Can she?

I take a deep, calming breath, and ask, "How long have you been here?"

She can't give me a yes or no answer to the question, and she looks at me in abject confusion.

"Have you always lived here?"

She nods, eyeing me cautiously.

"You have always lived in this room?"

Again, she nods.

"You never go out?"

Confusion again. She nods, and then shakes her head, and I realise the ambiguity of the question.

"Do you ever go out?" Of course she does, because I saw her out there. I chased her. I thought she was Katie. Once a day. I remember the words from earlier. *Once a day.*

"Have you ever been into the village?" I ask.

She shakes her head, pleased with herself that she can answer this one easily.

"Never?"

She shakes her head again.

"Why?" I ask. I know that she can't answer this with a yes or no, but I have to ask. I need to know.

She looks at the floor beneath her chair and drags her foot back and forth.

"You can answer," I say. "It's okay."

She just keeps moving her foot, and then I realise, she is making a line in the dust below.

"The line? You don't go into the village because of the line?"

"The lines," she whispers.

There were two circles.

"You keep between the lines."

She nods ferociously.

"Keep between the lines. Yes, yes."

As much as I am thinking that I need to get out of here, and that I need to do it as soon as possible, I can't leave her here. She's been a prisoner in this room all of her life, this room and the space between the lines in the woods, anyway, and that is no kind of life. Not for anyone. Why though? Why has he kept her here?

"Why?" I ask weakly. "Why?"

"Danger, danger, danger, danger."

She repeats the word over and over until I raise my hand in a stop sign.

"It's dangerous for you outside of the lines?"

Again, she nods. "The men from the town would take me away."

"Has anyone tried to take you away?"

She looks around and seems to think for a minute.

"No. I don't see many people. When I see people, they run away. They usually run away. You didn't."

She gives me a shy smile. "You wanted to come with me. You wanted to come in here with me."

"I…" I am about to tell her that I wanted to find my girlfriend, that I thought she was Katie, but I stop myself. A plan starts to germinate in my mind.

"Yes," I say, returning her smile. "I want to be your friend. Do you have many friends?"

Her face is heartbreakingly sad.

"Me neither," I say, and I can say it with as much emotion as I do because it is true. "I don't really have any friends."

"Mean dog. Bad dog is your friend."

"Yes, Dexter is my friend. He's not really a bad dog, he tries to look after me. He didn't know…" I pause, quickly searching for the right words. "He didn't know what a good girl you are."

Her face beams like the sunlight she must rarely see.

"I am a good girl. I'm not a ghost."

"That's what they say about you though. That you are a ghost?"

She nods. They shout and scream and run.

"They think you are someone else. They think you are someone who was here a long time ago."

"Did she live here before I did?"

I feel such a deep pang when she says that. The thought that Roman had someone else holed up in here before Audrey.

"Near here. Not in your room."

Then I stop. What if Annabel was in this room? Before her body was found. Before her remains were found. Remains. That's what the article had said, remains found.

My breath has quickened, my heart gallops. I want to know what she knows.

"Where are your parents?" I ask, fumbling the words.

"I don't have any," she says flatly.

Her face doesn't show any kind of emotion, not like you might expect from a young person telling you that they are an orphan.

"What happened to them?"

"I never had any."

She says it in such a matter-of-fact way. I'm stunned into silence. I don't know what to say next.

"Roman found me," she says. "Under a wimberry bush."

Her face beams with pride, like this is some kind of epic achievement. I must have paled to the same colour that she is. I have to keep myself under control. I have to make the right decision, say the right thing.

I take a breath, and say, as softly as I can manage, "You are very special."

It's the magic word.

She gets up from her chair and comes back over to me.

She sits on the floor by my side. I could headbutt her, knock her out, get the hell out of here. What's been stopping me from trying to get out of these ropes and getting away anyway? It's her. I can't hurt her, and I can't just leave her here. I can't.

"You can untie me now," I say. "You're allowed."

I don't *ask* to be untied; I tell her that it is okay. I hope that I have said enough for her to want to help me, and that I have given her the right words to feel like it is alright to do so.

"Why?" she asks, and she sounds genuinely surprised.

"I don't like being tied up. Not really."

The answer seems to make sense to her. She nods and starts to unpick the knot on the rope around my wrists.

"You're a good friend," I say.

I keep smiling, all the time smiling, and all the time trying to work out how to get up to that hatch and get the hell out of here.

Chapter Fourteen

Once my wrists are untied it doesn't take me long to free my legs. My left hand still aches from where the leather strap of Dexter's lead ripped across it earlier. There's an angry red mark glaring out. Now there are savage bruises on my wrists where the rope dug into them. Exactly how long has it been since I was brought down here? I have no idea. Have they had Katie all this time? Is she upstairs somewhere in Blackheath's manor? Is there only a ceiling or a floor between us? I think about shouting, attracting her attention, but I don't want to scare Audrey. Not now, not after we have come this far.

"Thank you, Audrey. That feels so much better." I smile again, but I don't reach out to touch her. No pat on the arm, definitely no hug. Careful, Seb, slow and steady.

"Better?" she says.

"Better," I nod.

I stand up, stretch my legs and feel the tension in my muscles. I offer Audrey a hand to help her to her feet too. She can take it, or she can refuse, her choice.

She looks at me for a few seconds, and then takes hold of my hand, pulling herself up.

"Thanks," she says.

"That's what friends are for," I smile.

"What are friends for?" she asks, and my smile switches from fake to genuine. She doesn't know. She doesn't know that it's a saying. She doesn't know anything about friendship. She doesn't know anything about life. I can't imagine what it must have been like for her down here.

Playing poker, I have learned to keep my emotions under control, not to get worked up, angry, irritated, and not to show when I am exceptionally happy or unhappy. Over time, I have probably not only learned to control how I display my emotions, but also whether I even feel those emotions at all. I'm not exactly a machine, but I know how to keep my cool.

I've been tied up in a room with a weird girl that I suspect has been a prisoner here for eighteen years, yet I'm not immediately running for the exit. I'm planning, thinking, trying to get it right.

She sees me looking at the hatch again.

Very quietly, almost imperceivably, she says, "You can't go up there."

"It's okay. I'm allowed. And if you come with me, you are allowed too."

She looks at me, trying to unpick the puzzle. I wait while she thinks, not hurrying her.

"No," she says, firmly. "No."

I shake my head. My mask of calmness is about to slip. I need to be out of here before Blackheath comes back. I'm trying my best to help Audrey, and to get her to come with me, but if I can't then I can't. I'll make it to the village and call the police, and they can come out and pick her up. Fine. I've done my best here.

"Please. Come with me. Be my friend."

"Roman is my friend. I am not allowed to go up there unless Roman opens the door. It's dangerous. Danger, danger, danger."

With each word her voice becomes louder. I put my finger to my lips and pat my other hand against the air.

"Ssh, ssh, ssh."

The last thing I need is for Roman to come back before I have the chance to get out. I don't want her alerting him. I can't have that.

"Okay," I say. "Okay. I *am* allowed though, and I'm going to have to leave now."

The sadness in her eyes is devastating.

"I'll see you again soon. I promise." I actually mean it. I really do.

She shakes her head.

"No," she mouths dryly.

I have to focus on the hatch now, and on getting myself up and out.

There's nothing below the sealed opening that I can boost myself up on to get to the hatch. There's the chair in the middle of the room, a little table that looks like it might break if I stand on it, and Audrey's drawers. They look like my best option. I give them a tug away from the wall, and then squeeze in behind them to get them into position beneath the hatch door.

"No," Audrey shouts. "No. No. No."

"It's okay, it's okay," I repeat as I move the drawers.

I'm committed now. I've set myself on this path and I'm not going to quit until I am out of here. This is it. I guess I'm all-in on this one.

"No!" she continues.

I get the drawers into position and start to climb up onto them. My hands make contact with the bottom of the hatch door, and I'm just about to push it open when it moves out of my reach. For a split-second I'm confused, but then I see

Blackheath's face looming over me. I've left it too long. I tried to save the girl, and now I am in the shit. I am deep, deep in the shit.

"Going somewhere?" His voice is full of malice.

I look down at Audrey below, who is still repeating, "*Nonononono*," and I try to keep my balance. I've got to make a quick decision now, no chance of thinking time. I either try to pull Blackheath down, or I wait for him to drop his ladder or whatever he has, let him in and then use it to make my escape. I'm not tied up anymore, what's the worst he can do? He's, what, fifty something? He's big, sure, but I'm youngish, fit and strong. Reasonably strong, anyway. Either way, I think I have a chance. I don't have to do much damage, just enough to be able to get a head start on him and get away.

If I make the wrong decision, if I pull him down and then none of us can get out, what then? I have to let him lower the ladder.

"No," I say. "No."

I lower myself back to the floor and step back.

Audrey stops her repetitive drone and flings her arms around my waist in a hug. I wasn't expecting that. I don't need her clinging onto me now. I pat her hand gently and she lets go.

"Very sensible," Roman says.

I was expecting some kind of wooden steps, like the fold-down kind you get in a loft, but instead he flops a wooden-runged rope ladder over the edge of the hole.

It suddenly hits me that the air coming in through the hatch is icy cold. We are not in Blackheath's manor. We are in the woods. This hatch is sunk somewhere beneath the needle-carpeted ground.

I'm distracted by the thought, but not for long enough that it disrupts my plan.

"Friends," I whisper to Audrey and she nods, a smile blossoming on her face.

Roman has to turn his back on me as he climbs down the ladder. It sways slightly, but I can tell he has made this climb so many times before. He is steady despite the movement, but now is my chance. I break away from Audrey, race to the bottom of the ladder and tug as hard as I can on Blackheath's legs. I have my arms around his knees, trying to buckle him, unbalance him and drop him to the floor. I flash a quick look over to the girl, but her hands are over her eyes. She's not going to be any help to me. Not at all.

"Stupid, stupid man," Roman shouts. He kicks out at me, but I arch my body so that his feet meet only air. "You're not getting out of here. Not ever."

But I am. I am getting out to find Katie. I am getting out to find Dexter. I am getting out to find help for Audrey. Somewhere at the bottom of the list I am getting out for me. I have spent the past few years being an asshole, now it's time for me to do something good.

"You're special," Audrey says, and I know that she is aiming it at me. It gives me the boost I need to give one final heave at the hefty man on the ladder and pull him to the ground. On the way down, he clips his head against the corner of the drawer unit. He's not knocked out, but he's dazed, and it buys me some time.

"You too," I say. "Come with me?"

"No," she replies. She walks over to Blackheath and crouches by his side, running her hand over his hair. Despite what he is and whatever he has done, she still has dogged loyalty to him.

I give her a final glance, and heave myself up the ladder, trying to stop it from twisting, trying not to fall.

The cold air of the woods slaps me in the face, but it wakes me up in a way that I need. I have to focus; I have to keep moving. Where am I? I have no idea. All around me, all I can see is the same scene – trees, gaps between trees, shrubs, ground. Nothing to tell me which way I should head.

The ladder is attached to the top of the hatch. It's been buried under dirt on the woodland floor, concealed here for however long this place has existed. I can't imagine what it has been like for Audrey down there. I want to pull the ladder up so that Roman doesn't come after me, but I want to leave it for Audrey to come up if she finds the strength. I have the feeling that Blackheath could use the drawers to climb up if he wanted to anyway. I leave the ladder, and I start to run.

I make an arbitrary decision about which way to head. I need to get to the village. How wide is the estate? What will happen if I run the wrong way? If I find the line, I can follow that round until I get to the track, I can use that to get myself in the right direction. If I get to the cabin, I can take the car. To think I was going to go straight to Blackheath. To think I was going to ask him to help me find Katie.

Katie, Katie, Katie. Is she still at the manor? Has he got her tied up there, just like he had me in the bunker? Or worse, is it worse? I can't let myself think about that. I can't think that way.

I run, between the trees, over the dirt and pressed pine needles. I have been running for only a few minutes when I feel a sharp cutting sensation on my ankle, and I fall sprawling only the floor.

"Shit!" I say it quietly, under my breath, even though I want to scream the word.

I know immediately what it is. I've stepped into a snare. I try to keep still, lower my hand down to loosen the noose and release the trap. Sitting on the floor, panting from the run, and the pain in my leg, I hear heavy footfalls, and they are heading in my direction.

"Shit, shit, shit."

I rip the snare open and slip my foot through. The wire caught on my sock, beneath my jeans, they must have risen enough as I ran to let the wire find a juicy target point. Just my luck. I can't stay here feeling sorry for myself or checking the damage, I have to grit my teeth and motor on. I keep as still as I can while I try to scan for the source of the sound of the pursuer, just a few seconds, just to see how far away he is.

He's not far away at all.

I can't hide here. There's nowhere to conceal myself. The trees are thin and spindly, the shrubs are too patchy, too small. This is going to hurt, but I have to keep moving.

I drag myself up and force my legs to run. Run, run, run.

The sound of an angry, murderous Blackheath leaping after me gives me more than enough motivation to follow my own advice.

"You can't get away. There's nowhere to go," he hollers.

I save my breath for the race. My ankle throbs and tries to resist my commands, but I believe my life depends on this, and perhaps Katie's does too.

The land slopes downwards a little, and the run is easier for a few hundred feet. It gives me a chance to put some space between us, but he's still behind me, still pounding after me. I don't recognise where I am yet. I have no clue. At the bottom of the dip, I choose to stay on the flat, rather than trying to run up the hill on the other side. Still, everything looks the same; still Roman is on my trail. I've got to outrun him, it's my only chance.

My ankle throbs, my heart thunders. I wish I'd spent more time at the gym, but my adrenaline is strong enough to drive me on. Adrenaline, fear, determination, a cocktail of all three. Whatever it is, I run, and I run.

For an older man, Blackheath is in remarkably good shape. I can hear him behind me now. I can't turn around to look, but I know he is there.

I push myself, trying to pick up speed, but I feel a swipe though the air behind me as he reaches out to grab me and pull me down.

How has he caught me? What the hell do I do now?

"No!" I shout and try to find the reserves deep within me to draw from.

It's no use. Two more steps and he has me. He leaps forward and pushes me to the ground. He's on top of me, throwing punches at my face. I raise my arms to protect myself, trying to get him off me, trying to stop him from using me as a punchbag. What do I do now?

One heavy fist lands, then the other, left then right, smashing into my face.

"I told you that you were not leaving alive. As soon as you saw her, it was over for you."

A quick thought flashes into my mind. Do what they don't expect you to do. Don't always take the predictable line. I start to laugh.

He lands one more punch, and then stops.

"What is there to laugh about?"

I don't reply. I keep laughing. There's blood streaming from my nose and I'm sure it must be broken, but I laugh and I laugh.

"Shut up," he says. "Shut up."

"I didn't even know who she was," I say. "I was too stupid to work it out until you had me trapped down there. All this was for nothing. For nothing." I keep laughing, hoping like hell that it will throw him.

"Shut the fuck up," he says and drops his fist one more time into my face.

I let go of Blackheath. He's going to keep punching me anyway and pretty soon he's going to knock me out, or worse. I have to do something. The world is swimming in front of my eyes. The woods have become a blur. I wish I had a pocketknife or something useful, anything. All I have is…

I plunge my right hand into my jeans pocket and grab Katie's crucifix. Heavy, warm silver. I catch hold of the cross between my fingers, draw it out, and raise it. As hard as I can, I ram the longest point towards Blackheath's face and into his eye.

He yowls in pain, and clutches at himself, for a moment stopping the onslaught of blows.

I try to move. I thought this would be my chance to get out from under him and get away. He is too heavy, too strong, and if he wasn't angry enough before, he certainly is now.

"You stupid b-" he starts to talk, but before he finishes the word he falls forwards, almost flat onto my face. I don't understand at first what has happened.

"Audrey?" I say, or at least try to say. I have no breath left to speak, and my mouth is filled with blood.

It's not Audrey. I hear the rumbling growl before I see the black fur and white teeth.

"Dexter. Oh shit, Dexter."

Dex is tearing at Blackheath, his teeth are deep sunk into his arm now, scissoring back and forward and Roman is thrashing, trying to get him off.

I shove into the ground and free myself, rolling out from under the man.

I could get Dexter to stop, but why? I kick at Blackheath, keeping him on the ground, letting Dexter continue.

"Good boy," I say. "You're a good dog."

I still need to get away. I've got to get to my car. I stick my hands back into my pockets, I don't have my keys. I should have realised before now. I don't have my keys.

Either I left them in the cabin, or Blackheath took them from me. Shit. I have to get to the village then. I have to go, and I have to go now.

I don't make the same mistake twice. I unfasten my belt, put my foot with its bleeding ankle onto Roman's back, and yank his arms behind him. I tie them together the best I can, tightening the strap as much as possible. This is not just about securing him, this is payback. I want to strap his feet together too, but I don't have anything else.

Dex's collar. Of course. I don't want to stop Dex from his well-executed mauling, not until we are ready to go, so I reach around him, and awkwardly unfasten his red leather collar. Then I move down to Blackheath's legs and bind it around them, drawing them together. It's an expensive collar and it's strong. Blackheath won't be breaking free of that in a hurry.

All this time, Blackheath has been shouting at Dexter to stop, and throwing expletives at me. I don't care. My only focus is on getting away, getting help, saving Katie, saving Audrey. Now I have Dexter. Dexter is fine, and the fact that Dexter is fine gives me hope.

Chapter Fifteen

I run, Dexter runs by my side, and we don't stop until we get to the door of *The Woman in the Woods*.

I don't imagine that I'm going to be welcomed with open arms after the way I left things with Carla earlier in the week, but I expect that will change quite quickly.

I'm aware of how I must look. I've been beaten and bound, and probably drugged, and I have run through the woods to get here. I am covered in sweat, in blood, my jeans are filthy and ripped, and I have this grimy, collarless dog by my side.

I push through the entrance, and almost collapse onto the bar.

"Carla. Call the police."

She stares at me. Everyone in the pub stares at me. Not in the same way that they did last time I was here. Then, I was an out-of-towner, unwelcome and unwanted. Now, I don't think they know what to make of me.

The barmaid stands almost gape-mouthed, as I say again. "The police. Call the police."

Dexter has fallen to the floor at my feet. It's been a long run for him too. A tough day. That's quite the understatement.

I'm exhausted, but I still have a sense of urgency.

"Carla."

"What the…"

"I think I found your niece. Also, Katie, my girlfriend has gone missing. Roman Blackheath tried to murder me, and I've tied him up and left him in his woods somewhere. So, please. Call the police."

Her mouth does fall open, as she tries to take in everything I just told her. She picks up the phone, and hands it to me.

"You'd better explain it to them," she says, and then she rings the last orders bell. "Everyone out. OUT. NOW."

The other customers are going to hate me if this happens every time I come in here.

I tap in 9-9-9 and wait to be connected to the police, trying all the while to think of exactly how I am going to phrase this. Clearly the explanation that I just gave to Carla isn't going to cut it with the law.

I try to keep calm.

When the friendly, professional officer answers, I tell him everything.

"I'm staying in a cabin on Blackheath Estate, Culloton. My girlfriend went missing while I was walking the dog this morning." I think it was this morning. I hope it was. "I went to look for her, and I was…" I pause and think. "I was attacked and tied up. I think I was probably drugged. I woke up in an underground room, also on Blackheath Estate. The person who attacked me was the owner of the estate and the cabin we were staying in, Roman Blackheath. Um…there was a girl in the bunker too, and I believe she was the daughter of Annabel Harford…"

"Annabel Harford?"

"Yes, Annabel Harford. The daughter of."

There's a short silence at the other end of the line.

"Where are you now, sir?" the policeman says.

"I'm in *The Woman in the Woods* public house. My phone…Blackheath took my phone, but I came here the other night and it seemed…I don't know. I didn't know where to go really."

Carla pours vodka for both of us, sets mine down in front of me and drains her own. Then she pours out a bowl of water for Dex before refilling her glass.

"I got out, anyway. I tried to get her out too, the girl, Audrey, but…she wouldn't come. The bunker is…er, left, I guess south-west, of the cabin on the Blackheath Estate. She's probably still there, I don't know." I'm starting to lose the plot now. My words are a garbled flow. "Sorry. I tied Blackheath up. He attacked me when I was running away, so I tied him up. He's, er, between the bunker and…shit I don't know. Oh man… I thought he was going to kill me, I had to get away. I had to get help. He has Katie. I'm sure she's in the manor. Someone is there with her; I don't know who. Please. You have to help."

I'm struggling to speak, but I want to get it all out. I don't know what else to say.

Those ties can't hold Blackheath for long. I was thinking about getting away and getting help, they weren't meant to be a long-term solution. I should have ended him when I had the chance. That's not me though. I wouldn't do that. I couldn't.

I down the vodka and wait to see what the officer says. I can hear the scratch of pen on paper; he's getting all the information down.

"Okay," he says. "That's quite a story."

He doesn't believe me. Oh shit, he doesn't believe me and I have to save Katie and…

"I'll send it through to dispatch. We'll have a car over at the manor as soon as we can. Are you able to stay there?"

"Can I stay here until the police come?" I ask Carla, and she nods.

"Yes," I say into the phone. "Yes. But please. You have to hurry. Please get Katie."

"Can I take some details from you quickly, sir?"

"Sure, of course."

I give him my name and confirm that this is the best phone number to currently reach me on, and he gives me a crime reference. His response is short and sweet, which I take as a good thing. He wants to pass the information on to the action team, or whatever they are called. Someone is going to get out to Katie. I hope it's not too late.

After I hang up the phone, I raise the glass of vodka that Carla has replenished for me. She has come around to my side of the bar, and she's sitting next to me, drinking her share too.

"Audrey. How? Why? After all this time. I don't understand any of this. None of it makes sense." Carla shakes her head.

"She, Audrey, said that she was found, that Blackheath found her under a wimberry bush. I remembered what you said, about why they were there. Was there anything going on between Annabel and Blackheath?"

"No, he was always, you know, introverted. He stayed out there in the manor on his own. He didn't mix with the villagers, and well, we have never really cared. Not then, and not now. She didn't know him. None of us did. None of us do."

"Are you sure? Would she have told you if…?"

"Annabel was in love with the man who abandoned her. After he left, she wasn't interested in anyone else. She did go out to Blackheath's estate, but, no, I'm sure there was nothing like that. Not from her side anyway." She seems to be considering something before she takes another mouthful of vodka.

"I read about what happened. The other night, after I met you. I'm so sorry. I was an asshole. In general, I am quite often an asshole. I'm sorry. It must have been terrible."

"Losing them? Yes. Of course. Not knowing what had happened to them, that was the worst part. My niece missing for all those years. I thought she was dead, of course I did, and she's been…"

"Hidden, I suppose. Kept prisoner. I wish I could have brought her out with me. I tried, I really did, but…"

She nods. "I understand. The police will collect her now, and…" She stops. "Well, I don't know what. She isn't the little girl that went missing anymore. I don't even know where to start. What am I meant to do?"

I shake my head.

"I'm sorry. You must be absolutely fraught worrying about your girlfriend. Are you sure Blackheath had her?"

"He spoke to someone on a walkie, like I said. I'm sure they were talking about her. That he had her. I don't understand why though."

"You were out with the dog? When she went missing?"

"Yeah. Katie was going to have a bath. As far as I could tell she did that, and then, who knows?"

"This is…it's too much for me to take in, I'm sorry."

I put my hand onto hers. "Thanks for letting me wait here."

"It's fine," she said. "You found Audrey. I know you're worrying about Katie, but I am just trying to work out what I say to her when they bring her back here."

I let out a little sigh. How do I explain how the girl is now? She seems, I don't know, physically well, but psychologically, she's definitely suffered from being alone. She's been through so much, and the bunker is all she's ever known. That and the abject fear of everything outside of those two lines drawn in ashes on the ground; fear that she has been programmed to feel. Blackheath must have started to ingrain that feeling in her from such an early age. It's all she has known, there's been no one to tell her otherwise. It wasn't the lines themselves that keep her in, it was the fear of what they represented. It was the idea that scared her, not the facts.

"I have to get out there. I have to find Katie."

"The police are on their way. Let them handle it. There's nothing you can do. Not right now."

I can't believe her words. I could go down to the manor, I could. I should. As if reading my mind, Carla shakes her head.

"Wait, Seb. Please. We both have to wait."

"I'm always so useless. So absolutely useless. I have made so many mistakes."

Carla lets me rant away to myself. I can tell her thoughts are elsewhere, but I don't have it in me to comfort her when all I can think about is Katie.

Dexter sits up and rests his head against my leg and I gently stroke him wondering how long it will be until the police get here, and who they will bring with them when they arrive.

Chapter Sixteen

After what feels like an eternity, but is actually closer to an hour, there's an insistent knocking on the door.

Through the bay window, I can see both a police van and car. They took me seriously, at least.

Carla and I look at each other, and I offer her a hug. She accepts, and then we drop from the stools and head to the door.

"Have you got her?" I ask, before the officer or Carla can say anything.

Carla steps aside to let the female policewoman into the room. She ushers her to a table and the three of us sit.

"We have Katie," the officer says.

I almost collapse as the relief explodes within me. Carla grabs hold of my arm to steady me, and I lean against the doorframe, unable to bear my own weight.

"Is she okay? Has he hurt her? Was she…?" I can't stop myself. "Where is she? Can I see her?"

"I need to take her to the station so that we can ask her some questions, but, yes, you can see her. She seems…mostly fine, yes."

"Mostly fine? I –"

"What about Audrey?" Carla interrupts. "Where's Audrey? Have you found her?"

"We haven't been able to locate the bunker yet, but a team are searching the estate. As soon as we have any information, I will let you know. I'll need to take your number and your details."

"Of course. Yes." Carla passes on her phone number, full name and confirms that she lives here, above *The Woman in the Woods*. The officer gives a wry smile at the name.

"It was in honour of my sister. Audrey's mother." She shrugs, seeming not to know what else to say.

"And Blackheath? Did you find him? Have you arrested him? He wanted to kill me. He tried to kill me."

"There was no sign of Roman Blackheath at the manor…"

"He was in the grounds. I tied him up. After he attacked me, I…"

"Yes sir, I know what you told control. We haven't been able to find Mr Blackheath yet. Our team are working on tracking him. We believe that he could be a dangerous man, and we are putting all of our efforts into finding him."

"And Audrey?" Carla says.

"Yes, into finding both of them."

I take a breath, and ask, "Can I see her?"

The policewoman nods, and gestures to the door.

I jump up and run out, peering into the back of the police car, looking for Katie.

She is there, an orange blanket wrapped around her shoulders, like a little old woman in a shawl.

"Oh shit, shit Katie. You're alright! I was so worried. Oh shit. Are you okay? You are okay?" I ramble again, trying to reach in to hold her, wondering if I am allowed to do this while she's in a police car, but really, I am past caring.

"Katie, what happened? Did he hurt you?"

She reaches up to me, and pulls me into the seat next to her, holding on to me for all she is worth.

"I'm okay. I'm fine, really. I'm fine. Ssh."

I'm crying, but she looks unbelievably calm.

"They didn't hurt me. No one hurt me. I didn't even know what was going on until the police turned up. I was bored. The internet was down. I couldn't get a signal on my phone, so..." She shrugs. "I wanted to get it sorted out before you came back. I knew you weren't in a hurry, so I figured I had time."

"Oh Katie. Did they tell you what happened? What happened to me?"

"Not really. You're okay though? You look like hell."

"I feel like I just got back. I've been tied up, drugged, beaten, and I found out about that ghost…"

"What?"

She stares wide-eyed and stunned.

I start to explain, running through the whole story again. I tone it down for Katie. She doesn't need all the details that I gave to Carla and the officer.

The policewoman comes to the side of the car.

"We need to get to the station now, sir."

"Can I go along with Katie?" I ask, and then I remember Dexter, lying in the pub. "Shit. The dog."

I look at Katie and then at the officer.

"We will need you to come to the station, Mr Archer. There are a few questions that we need to ask you too."

I'm still thinking about Dexter, and the words don't sink in immediately.

"Maybe Carla will let him stay here," I suggest.

"You can bring him along. No problem. As long as he is well behaved?"

"He's the best. I swear he's the absolute best."

They have questions for me. Of course they would. It makes sense that they would need to take a statement. I keep my cool, run into the pub and call Dex. He clambers to his tired feet and follows me to the car. He soon perks up when he sees Katie. After a gentle licking of her face, I get him to sit between us.

"Katie…" I start to speak.

The tears are streaming down her face. It's her turn to cry now.

I reach over Dex and gently place my hand onto her moist cheek.

"Hey, hey. Everything's going to be okay. You're safe now…"

Chapter Seventeen

At the police station, there are more questions for me, and more questions for Katie. We are taken into two separate rooms, and I tell the story of what happened yet again.

"And why did you not bring Miss Harford with you when you left the, as you call it, *'bunker'*?"

"I was worried about Katie. I thought Blackheath had her somewhere. All I could think about was getting out of there and saving my girlfriend."

"With no thought as to your own safety, or that of the girl who you believed had been locked in that room for eighteen years?"

"Yes, I was thinking of my safety. I was thinking that if I stayed there *he* would probably kill me. Blackheath told me that I was never leaving that room. He was either going to imprison me too, or worse."

"And yet he left you alone with the girl."

I might as well be tied to a chair again for this interrogation.

"I suppose he underestimated me. I was drugged, he had beaten me. I was bound at the hands and feet and there was no ladder. I'm sure he thought I wasn't going anywhere.

Maybe because she had never escaped, he thought that I couldn't either. When you find him, you can ask him."

The tape is recording, but the man asking the questions is still writing notes. I swear he is doing it to make me more nervous.

"I don't know what you want me to say. Everything I did, it was self-defence"

"I just want to be very clear about what happened. You don't have a witness, apart from your dog. This woman, well, as far as I know, she might not even exist. Your girlfriend went to Blackheath's manor because your internet was out, and meanwhile you managed to get kidnapped, escape from an underground prison and attack your alleged captor, who just happens to be the man you are renting your holiday cabin from." He looks down at the pad. "Yet you leave the girl in the 'bunker'" He stresses the final word again. He seems to somehow find it amusing.

I shake my head and look down at the table. For once, I don't know what to say. I don't know how to put together the information I have to make a balanced decision on how I should react. I am lost. I thought I was doing the right thing, and now, this.

"Your girlfriend was never in any kind of peril. She was drinking tea and checking her Instagram with one Mr Cawcroft, who I believe you met on Monday evening."

"Yes but, I didn't know it was him. He said that he was Roman Blackheath."

"Perhaps you misheard. You had driven a long way. You were tired. Had you been drinking then, just like you have today?"

"I've had some vodka. I was waiting for the police to arrive at *The Woman in the Woods*. I was going out of my mind."

The interviewer writes this down, and I make a mental note to choose my words more carefully.

"Carla poured me a drink and I drank it."

"What is your relationship with Ms Frampton?"

"Who, sorry?"

"Carla Frampton. What is your relationship with her?"

"I met her on Tuesday evening. Katie and I went for a drink in the pub. The locals started to tell us about this ghost story, about 'The Woman'. Carla set us straight. I'm afraid I didn't make a good first impression."

"So, you knew about the missing child?"

"Yes. I mean, no. I didn't know she was still missing. I thought the woman and the child had both died. I looked it up on the internet when we got back to the cabin."

"You did have internet access then? On Tuesday?"

"Then, yes." I am getting frustrated. I don't see the point of all these questions.

"Very well. Okay."

There's a knock on the door of the interview room, and a policeman pops his head in.

"We've found them," he says.

The interviewing officer gives him the thumbs up, and I let out a huge sigh.

"He's in bad shape, but..." The policeman at the door shrugs. "It all seems to be as Mr Archer here has told us. The girl's talking, and Blackheath, well, he will."

"Looks like your ghost girl has given you a lifeline."

The interviewing officer closes his notebook and stops the tape with a firm click.

I was a suspect? In what? Not her disappearance, surely. She's been down there since I was, well, too young to be able to abduct anyone anyway. I'm not sure what I was meant to have done, but the officer is already standing. I swear he looks almost disappointed that she has been found and he can't interrogate me further.

I want to be out of Culloton as soon as possible, once we've been told that we are free to go. One of the officers offers to give us a lift back to the cabin. I don't want to stay there a moment longer than we need to. Katie and I duck into the cabin and scoop all of our belongings into our cases. I quickly feed Dex, who has remained patiently quiet despite the fact that he must be starving by now, and throw his bed and bowls into the back of the car.

Dex, the good, good boy jumps into the back, and Katie and I silently strap on our seatbelts.

I take one final look at the cabin, and then turn the car towards the track and drive.

Before we leave Culloton, I pull up outside *The Woman in the Woods*. The door is shut, the pub is still closed, so I knock and wait.

Carla comes to the window and peers out at us. When she clocks that it's Katie and I, she moves to the door and unbolts it. On the doorstep she looks up and takes an audible deep breath.

"Going to have to change that sign now," Carla says, trying to smile.

I offer her a hug and she accepts it, before moving to the side to let us in.

We sit, but there's no vodka this time, for me or her.

"They're keeping Audrey at the hospital for now," she says. "She's in a state of shock, doesn't have a clue what's going on." Carla shakes her head and I think she's about to start crying, but she manages somehow to hold it back.

"It's going to take time, but I'm sure that things are going to be so much better for her now," I say.

I want to warn her, to say something about how attached she was to Roman, and how she didn't want to leave him. I don't know how to form the words. I don't know what good they will do. The hospital and Carla will both help Audrey to get over what has happened, perhaps it is best to say nothing, and let them heal together.

"She looks so much like her mother." Carla's voice grows smaller as she says this.

What must it be like to grieve for the loss of someone that you love and then have a part of them return? She's lost her sister, but now she has found Audrey, her niece. I found her. And I wasn't even looking. You could look at it one of two ways: I was either very lucky, or very unlucky. Seeing the hope and happiness that having Audrey back has brought to Carla, I know that whatever I went through had to be worth it.

Chapter Eighteen

We say our goodbyes to Carla, and Katie promises to keep in touch. I know she will. She'll want to know how the girl is getting on, not out of a sense of morbid curiosity or nosiness, but because she genuinely cares. That's just the way she is. Katie is an angel, she really is.

Back on the road, we sit without speaking. It's a reflective quietness, rather than one of the awkward, uncomfortable silences that I have been far too used to sharing with Katie.

We travel that way for almost an hour, before it hits me.

"Hey."

I suddenly remember that I have Katie's necklace in my pocket. I take the steering wheel in my left hand, although the skin is still aching across my palm. I reach into my right pocket with the other hand.

"I almost forgot."

I hand it over to her.

"Well," she says, holding it up. "What the hell happened to this?"

"I kind of used it as a weapon. I didn't have anything else on me, and I tried to jam it into Blackheath's eye."

There's nothing like blunt honesty, is there?

"That's disgusting." She pauses, and then says. "My mum would have been happy to help."

I curl my lips into a smile.

"She would," I say. "She would."

Katie reaches into the glove compartment and pulls out a pack of wet wipes. She sits, dabbing away at the blood and dirt on the chain. Despite what I just told her, she fastens the chain around her neck. I pat her gently on the thigh and we drive on in silence again for a couple of miles, both lost in our own reflection.

Katie is the first to speak. "What do you think will happen to Audrey?"

"I really don't know. Carla will do her best for her, I'm sure. But after all that time locked away, can she ever have a normal life?"

"At least she's out. I can't imagine what it must have been like for her."

"It's all she's ever known. He took her down there when she was a toddler, and brainwashed her. The weirdest thing was that she didn't want to leave. When I wanted to take her out of there with me. She wanted to stay. She wouldn't leave him."

"Do you think he…" She doesn't complete the sentence, but the look of disgust on her face tells me what she is thinking. I don't have an answer, so I shake my head.

"I don't know."

"All these years though. And no one saw her before now."

"Apart from the locals, who were convinced she was a ghost."

"Ironic isn't it? *The Woman in the Woods*. Shit. How awful for Carla. How awful for both of them." She shakes her head and runs her fingers through her hair.

"Being abducted and almost murdered was pretty bad for me too," I say.

She nods and puts her hand onto my leg.

"Kind of puts everything into perspective."

I take a deep breath, and I decide to say what it was that I was thinking about, spill out all the thoughts I had when I didn't know where Katie was.

"I know one thing, Pie. I never want to lose you. I'm sorry I let things fall apart like they did. I haven't been there with you often enough. I've never been around for you. Even today, I wanted my own space. I wanted time with

Dexter. I wanted time for myself. I've been selfish. I've been such an asshole"

"But I have too," she says, her voice equally as earnest as my own. "I wanted that bath. I was looking forward to just an hour without having you around." She looks away, bites her lip. "I don't mean…"

"Yes, you do, we both do. We both need time alone. Time to ourselves."

"But we need the time together too. The balance."

I nod. "And it only took nearly being killed by a kidnapper and potential murderer for us to find that out. Cheaper than couples' therapy, eh?"

I'm focussing on the road, and I can't see her roll her eyes, but I know she is doing it.

"How long are you going to play on that one?" she says with a dry laugh. "I could have been killed too, you know. I was in the murderer's lair, sitting in his living room, using his Wi-Fi."

I laugh too. Despite everything, I laugh. What else is there to do?

"I promise that in future we will spend more time together, and when we need to, or even when we want to, that we will spend time apart."

"Pinkie promise, Bun Bun?"

"I pinkie promise, Katie Pie."

My face throbs when I smile, there's a split on my lip, and I'm lucky to still have all of my teeth.

"And Katie?"

"Yes?"

"From now on, I think I will plan our holidays."

She slaps my leg, playfully, and I glance over to catch sight of her smile.

The love of my life. She really is.

I have been an asshole, but not anymore.

Not anymore.

Dear Reader,

Thank you for reading **"The Woman in the Woods"**.

If you have enjoyed this book, please consider leaving a review on Amazon and/or Goodreads. Reviews help readers to discover books, and help authors to find new readers. It would mean a lot to me if you would take a few minutes to leave a review.

If you would like to find out more about new releases and special offers, including information about the rest of this series, please sign up to my mailing list. I'm currently giving away a free full-length novel to everyone who signs up. Visit **jerowney.com** for details.

Best wishes
J.E. Rowney